Constellations of Fate

The Orion Dynasty Book 6

Ck Franco

Prologue

The night was never silent. Beneath the glittering skyline, shadows whispered of betrayals long buried and debts still unpaid. The Orion Brotherhood had always been more than men of power and wealth—it was a bond carved from blood, sacrifice, and secrets too heavy for the world to know.

But the universe is patient, and fate is merciless. The stars that once guided them now trembled, as if warning of the fracture that would change everything. Somewhere in that endless dark, unseen hands moved pieces on a board older than empires.

And on this night, a truth began to rise—one that would either bind the Brotherhood forever... or burn it to ash.

"The stars are not bound by the darkness that surrounds them—they burn because they must, and because someone, somewhere, needs their light."

— Anonymous

Blurbs

Five ruthless billionaires.
Five forbidden loves.
One brotherhood destined to break.

The Orion Brotherhood was built on loyalty and blood. But when betrayal strikes from within, every secret, every love, every vow is tested.

Caius, Lucien, Darius, Orion, and Silas must fight not only for survival—but for the women who dared to love them.

In this explosive finale, passion collides with power, and fate burns brighter than the stars.

For those who carried scars in silence, who fought battles unseen, and who still chose love over fear. This is for every soul who ever believed that even in the darkest night, stars can be reborn. To my readers—you are the constellation that guided this journey. This ending belongs to you as much as it belongs to them.

Contents

Flames in the Dark

At midnight, the city's skyline glistens behind panes of glass, the stars above barely visible beyond a haze of urban glow. Caius's skyscraper rises—black marble and steel, each shadowless corner a testament to wealth and dominance, a fortress that broods over the sleeping heart of the city. Among the elite, it is legend: a sanctum no force could crack, its security fears whispered about in private lounges, its boundaries set like the edge of a sanctuary. But tonight, the myth shatters.

With no warning, thunder erupts from the lobby. The impact rattles the veins of the building. Glass splinters rain like autumn hail, jagged confetti cascading across the onyx floor. The acrid stench of burning ozone—electrical wires cut and catching fire—fills the reception. Sirens scream, sharp and unnatural, as masked intruders pour through breaches where reinforced doors once gleamed.

Through the north corridor, the hum of quiet night work is replaced by chaos. Seraphina, steps from her office, halts as the world behind her convulses. Shots crack through the air, more sound than sense. A flash—one reinforced panel blown back—throws her into a ragged dance between survival and fate. Shards of marble bite the side of her neck. Her lungs stutter as she slams to the ground, concrete cold beneath her palms. Then a searing pain—a bullet rips past her arm, heat and fire, blood blooming across her skin. The taste of iron coats her tongue as she pulls herself behind an overturned sculpture, clutching the wound, pulse thundering.

Outside, chaos boils. Caius's security, sleek and trained, pull pistols from holsters and unleash bullets toward advancing figures indistinguishable behind black masks. Each footfall, each yell, is swallowed by the shriek of alarms and the staccato echo of gunfire ricocheting down marble halls.

Two guards in midnight blue dart into the hailstorm. Their gloved hands grip Seraphina's shoulders, dragging her low through smoke and dust. The world becomes kaleidoscopic—flashing muzzle flares, booted feet, the rotten sting of cordite. As bullets thud into walls, one guard pushes Seraphina behind a toppled bronze statue, yelling above the din.

"You breathe? Stay with me! Eyes here! That's it, hold pressure—"

She presses trembling fingers to her forearm, vision swimming. Her skin sticks slick to the marble, the world shrinking to the sound of her own ragged breath.

Downstairs, the main doors shudder open. Caius forces through, the tail of his dark coat flaring behind him, hair mussed, eyes narrowed with a violence cold and focused. He barely registers the trembling staff pressed flat against velvet walls. His world narrows to blood and the choking bite of smoke. Shouts fade; gunfire sharpens in his ears. His empire—his monument to invulnerability—groans under the weight of a power it was never meant to resist.

The lobby once gleamed. Now the air is a fog of splintered glass, spent shells spinning on marble. Ancient canvases hang at crooked angles. The jagged scent of ozone and burnt leather twists Caius's gut. Past the smoking wreckage of a fallen chandelier, he sees—her.

Seraphina. Blood pools beneath her, her brown eyes glazed but alive. The curve of her jaw is set in stubborn resolve, her arm slick with dark crimson, her breath shallow.

He kneels hard, feeling the tremor in his own hands as he yanks off his jacket and wraps it tight around her forearm. His voice shakes—not with fear, but with a fury that wants to kill.

"What were you doing in the north corridor?" he demands, biting back the fear as he tries to stanch the bleeding. "Why weren't you in your office?"

She tries to smirk, but it warps into a wince. "Didn't realize I'd need a flak jacket for paperwork tonight, Caius. I saw the alarms. I—I thought security would hold them off."

His jaw flexes, the scar on his cheek flashing white. "They shouldn't have gotten through. No one gets through." He presses harder. "Don't move. You're losing blood fast."

She nods stiffly, eyes fluttering, her breath growing thinner.

Other guards weave past, barking into radios—shouts for medics, for lockdown codes. Caius's heart pounds, ice and hellfire, as he looks around: his fortress, the sanctuary he built from sweat and soul, reduced to trembling stone. Each whisper of gunfire in the distance becomes a memory of betrayal, each spatter of Seraphina's blood a burning indictment of his failures.

He can't afford failures. Not with Seraphina's life in the balance, not with the city's predators watching, vultures circling over the Brotherhood's shadow. For years, this building had been a promise—of safety, control, power absolute. The illusion fractures beneath his knees, fear crawling down his spine, shame burning behind his ribs.

Sirens fade into a hollow, frantic drumbeat. Seraphina sags against him, consciousness slipping. Her fingers curl in his sleeve.

"Don't leave me, Seraphina," he whispers, rough and desperate. "I'm here, I'm not going anywhere."

Outside, alarms continue to wail. The smell of smoke and burnt metal thickens. Caius holds Seraphina as her eyes flutter closed, gunfire still punctuating the night, his world reduced to blood, marble, and the broken certainty that nothing—not even his empire—is untouchable.

The quiet in the medical suite is shattered every so often by the beep of machines and the murmur of hushed voices behind glass doors. Clinical white light casts soft halos across the polished floor. A haze of antiseptic hangs in the air—sharp, sterile, edged by a faint mineral tang from saline. Shadows flicker and stretch along the walls as staff move in and out, their pale uniforms whispering like the retreating tide. Beyond these barriers, Caius sits, immovable, in the straight-backed chair drawn stubbornly close to Seraphina's bedside.

On the crisp sheets, Seraphina's skin is ghostly but alive. The wound across her forearm is ugly, freshly stitched—a ragged, swollen red against olive skin. She floats on the anesthetic fog, breath shallow under the oxygen mask, eyelids fluttering with half-formed dreams.

Caius's jaw is clenched so tightly it aches. He stares at her hand lying limp atop the blanket, every inch of him aching to replace the chill of the I.V. drip with the warmth of his touch. His rage pulses beneath his skin, barely masked by the measured stillness in his posture. He is a man built for control, tempered by decades of careful choices, and those choices have failed her tonight. The world outside believes this fortress unbreakable—an empire of glass and steel, guarded by a man who never flinches. Yet here, beneath security more intricate than the pulse of the city itself, blood stains the sheets and nothing is certain.

A doctor murmurs an update—blood loss stabilized, blood pressure rising, nothing to be done now but wait. Caius dismisses the words with a clipped nod, his voice low and dangerous as he issues rapid instructions to tighten surveillance, double guards, and comb the staff records. "Nobody enters this wing," he snaps, sending a junior aide into flight down the corridor. His hands, usually rock-steady, tremble against the cool edge of the metal rail when no one's watching.

He leans closer, his breath warming frostbitten fingers, studying Seraphina's pale lips as if willing color to return. Love, an old battle-scar, seeps through every line of his face—a vulnerability at odds with everything else about him. He smooths a stray lock of hair from her forehead, the gesture barely more than a whisper. He tries to quiet the frantic thrum in his chest, but the memory clawing up from the deep will not relent. He's seen rooms like this before: white lights, the perfume of blood and salt, the echo of a monitor's alarm cutting the air. He's lost too much already. His power, his cunning—none of it shields her now.

Seraphina stirs, lashes trembling, a gasp rippling through the silence.

"Caius?" Her voice is shredded, breath rasping through the mask. Panic flickers in her eyes as she tries to sit upright, only to falter against pain and the weight of linens.

"Easy. You're safe. You're safe, with me," he says, but fear cracks through the practiced calm.

Her gaze darts beyond—listening for phantom gunfire, lips forming the fragments of dread.

"Was anyone else—hurt?" Her hand twitches, desperate for news, her body rigid, every muscle braced for grief.

He lowers himself so their eyes align, knuckles brushing her cheek. "Everyone else is accounted for. Security contained it. You fought, Sera. You fought hard."

Her grip finds his sleeve, anchoring herself with what frail strength she has. "You shouldn't leave them unguarded." Her words catch; guilt sharpens her features, tears unshed.

"And I won't. But you come first—always." His tone is steel, but the promise shakes with what he cannot say aloud.

Doors hiss open. A nurse checks the drip. Caius doesn't flinch, doesn't move, not even when the nurse urges him back for a breath of air.

"She needs peace. And so do you—for her sake."

Caius's glare is silent fire. "She's not alone. Not while I breathe. Double the perimeter." The nurse, cowed, disappears into the bright-lit corridor, leaving only the chorus of machinery and Caius's thunderous heartbeat.

He stands, shoulders knotted, and paces one revolution around the bed. In a swift gesture, he calls up the secure line on his encrypted device.

"Lucien," he says, voice low and flint-hard, "call Darius, Orion, Silas. Brotherhood meets tonight. We're under assault. Whoever orchestrated this will bleed for it."

Static crackles as voices at the other end reply—fear, fury, and the echo of oaths exchanged.

Seraphina, drifting again, shivers beneath her blanket. Guilt etches lines into her brow, haunted by shadows of those imagined lost. Caius kneels beside her, fingers barely brushing the pulse in her wrist.

He lowers his head, whispers, "You're not leaving me. I'll raze the world before I let them take you."

The suite fills again with soft beeps, the glass walls reflecting two figures locked together against the night's ruin.

The Brotherhood gathers beneath the world, in a chamber buried so deep that the city's buzzing sirens can't seep through. Granite walls, polished until the candlelight and amber sconces gild their edges, swallow their reflections. The heavy, blackened oak table absorbs the weight in the room—the tremor in every jaw, the heat behind every glance. No one sits comfortably. Caius's knuckles remain white where they grip the chair, the dried cut across his hand a silent accusation. Darius's suit jacket is wrinkled at the elbow where restless fingers have tugged; Lucien's eyes alone move, shadows glinting over encrypted reports he hasn't yet shared. Orion lingers, barely resisting the urge to pace, every muscle primed like a loaded trap. Silas is stillness embodied—almost a shadow himself, but his gaze cuts icily over his brothers, cataloguing every twitch.

Caius's voice is different tonight. Every syllable carries the metallic aftertaste of alarm. He recounts Seraphina's wounds—the sound of reinforced glass splintering against gunfire, the way her body slumped behind the ruined statue, the blood that slicked the marble floor beneath her. Even now, each sentence claws through the memory. As he speaks, the room seems smaller, the table more coffin than council. The air is thick with a scent of sweat and fear clinging to expensive aftershave, tinged by the unwelcome staleness of a place meant for secrets.

Darius's fist slams the table hard enough to rattle the constellation emblems etched into the wood. The sound is startling; ancient dust shakes free from a velvet curtain. "How the hell did they get through?" His voice cracks, raw. "Our system was built for war, not show. I want names. I want the breach charted from login to bullet."

Lucien's hand, always steady, flickers over a console. Blue holographic light washes over grim eyes. "They hit in two waves. First took out outside comms, second breached after we lost main power. These patterns—military precision. My teams flagged three data pings from within our own firewall. Not Russian, not local. No digital fingerprint we can buy off." He flings a look toward Silas, then Orion. "This wasn't an amateur play. And it wasn't some zealot with a grudge."

Orion sweeps a hand through his hair, restless energy barely caged. "You're damn right it wasn't. This feels wrong. Too clean. We're either bleeding info..." His glare sharpens, voice colder. "Or someone inside's serving your blueprints as an entrée."

A pointed silence follows. Silas leans forward, the overhead 'stars' catching on the silver thread at his cuff. "I've seen this pattern. Not in the open—buried. Targeted threats. False tracers routed through our own security staff the past two months. My chief tracker turns up dead last week. I dismissed it as blowback from the Lissenti affair. I was wrong." He pulls in a breath through his teeth, voice dry as crushed glass. "Whoever's orchestrating this, they're watching us fight our shadows while they map our lungs."

"So we lock it down." Darius's eyes dart over each brother. "Every code, every channel, every guard's record and movement. If there's a rot inside, we'll smoke it out."

"I'll slice through the system logs for any sign of a ghost protocol," Lucien adds, words clipped, already turning over digital leads. "But it'll take time. This enemy hides in our mirror. We double teams on diagnostics. Silas and I will cross trace—two sets of eyes, no assumptions."

"I'll sweep the estate staff myself," Orion says, jaw clenched. "If there's a traitor in my hall, I'll drag them out before sunrise."

Wordless agreement hums in the flicker of glances—resolve forged in bruised pride and deeper wounds.

Caius stands, and the chair's scrape echoes in the chamber's drawn hush. The low hum of monitors, the faint tick of hidden machinery—these are the only witnesses now. Shadows stretch across his scarred face as he weighs their future. The Brotherhood's rules were once unbreakable laws. Enemies didn't hit at home; blood wasn't meant to spill onto the roots. Now, that illusion lies shattered, streaked over wan hospital sheets and slick marble. Protection feels as thin as glass, trust as frail as candlelight, and Caius envisions, for the first time, their empires devoured from within—children caught in crosshairs, wives used as leverage, secret chambers breached and laid bare beneath the city's lights.

He imagines the enemy's next move not as a distant raid, but as poison slipped into shared wine, or betrayal with the warmth of a brother's hand. The thought cracks something old and careful inside. Guilt gnaws at him—every overlooked security file, every blind spot permitted for the sake of harmony. He sees Seraphina's face pale as snow, her fingers twitching in unconscious pain. A leader is meant to shield his family—not awaken to their ruin.

He shoves down the fear, molds it instead into ice-cold purpose. Their brotherhood is on the line, not just their money or blackmail ledgers, but the core of who they are—what they've promised each other in blood and night and all those whispered oaths beneath constellations.

The chairs scrape back, one by one. Eyes meet without blinking. The Brotherhood will not flinch again.

Midnight's Shattered Truth

Night presses against the glass, cold and implacable, as the hum of Mariel's laboratory vibrates under a fluorescent hush. Rows of glass panels shimmer beneath stark LED light, separating her from her staff and the city outside—an aquarium of science, knowledge, and ambition that she has curated cell by meticulous cell. Medicinal herbs in the slender indoor garden tremble faintly with the ventilation's whisper. She stands alone before her secure terminal, her eyes tracing lines of coded data, brow furrowed as she waits for the final figures. Each keystroke is a familiar incantation until the screen flickers. An urgent message cuts across her day's equations:

URGENT—DATA BREACH DETECTED. WORLD CAST STATUS: COMPROMISED

Above the sterile clutter of holographic displays, the international science webcast blooms to life on every lab screen. But instead of her research—years distilled from sleepless nights and fierce intellect—there is a grotesque parody of her work scrolling for all the world to see. The numbers are wrong. The calculations are contradicted by simple logic, and the visuals are deliberately mangled. Is this sabotage or a nightmare? Her throat dries; every muscle tightens. A cold mineral taste blooms under her tongue.

She presses trembling fingers to the edge of her desk. The crisp, antiseptic scent of the lab is suddenly suffocating. Staff cluster by the observation window, voices fluttering in anxious, cross-currented hushes—do they see her panic? She claws back through her thoughts: every protocol, password, fail-safe. Had she missed something? Or is it someone?

A familiar, gnawing tightness seizes her chest as she pivots to her desk drawer. She fumbles through papers, old grant proposals, a photo of her as a wide-eyed postdoc—until her hand closes around a stark black envelope. The seal is unremarkable, but the weight of it hammers something primal at the base of her skull. She tears it open, heart pounding.

Inside, blocky type screams from the page:

If you care about your spotless reputation and your partner's life's work, comply with all demands. We control more than you think. Next time, you lose everything.

She reads it three times. The air chills, her pulse thrumming against the delicate constellation tattoo woven up her arm. Her hands—usually so steady with pipettes and code—shake so violently that she has to flatten them against the desk. The room recedes. Data corrupted, reputation poised for ruin, Lucien's name left twisting somewhere between threat and promise.

A wave of fear crashes over her. Not just for herself; for the empire that rises and falls nightly on these fragile digital ramparts. For Lucien—who wears control like armor but has shown her how thin and bruised the line is between power and annihilation. She wants to fight, to strike back, but her confidence is leaking away, cell by cell.

She squares her shoulders, barely holding it together. Behind the glass, her staff hovers—a sea of blue coats watching the ship's architect come undone. She pushes through the illuminated corridor, passing them with a wordless nod, their anxious eyes pressing into her back. She turns, almost hopeful that Lucien might materialize outside the glass, a sentinel in the glare. But she must seek him herself.

The secure suite beyond the laboratory is a capsule apart, its walls lined with softly glowing reliefs and the faint scent of steel and jasmine. Lucien waits by the digital map, his posture a monolith of composure.

"Lucien. I—" Her voice fights to be steady, but something raw seeps through.

He turns, eyes cold and calculating, gaze sliding from her face to the trembling envelope in her hands.

"They've sabotaged the webcast. My data's gone. Twisted—humiliated," Mariel forces out, barely above a whisper. "And there's more." She holds out the letter. "They want something from me. They'll destroy everything if I don't play along. Even you."

His fingers brush hers—cool, unflinching—as he takes the letter. He reads it in silence, his expression unreadable, except for the tightening of his jaw.

"Let me see it." Lucien steps to her workstation, scrolling through the destroyed public data, tracing digital footprints, every movement precise and predatory. The glow from the monitors paints him ghostly. Finally, he turns toward her, his voice cutting through the suspended quiet.

"Nobody will ruin you. Not them, not anyone. Do you understand? You say nothing of this to anyone outside of me. I'll find who did this." His hand lingers on her shoulder—rare, almost tender.

Mariel's breath shudders in her lungs. Being exposed, invaded, is a fear she has practiced brushing aside. But now—every circuit in her body is tuned to disaster.

"Lucien, what if it's someone in the lab? I can't look them in the eye. I can't—" She swallows hard. "They know everything. My work, my name..."

His tone is steel. "You trust me. Keep this secret. That's all I ask. I'll handle everything else."

Lucien's authority is rock—cold, relentless—and she clings to it. Her racing mind tries to conjure explanations, suspects, allies who might be traitors. But none of it fits.

He leaves, envelope clenched in his fist, a figure cut from calculated promise and quiet vengeance.

She sinks into the far corner, knees pulled up, arms wrapped tight. The glass reflects her double—a woman fierce and broken, confidence bleeding out under sterile lights as the storm rages on both sides of the glass. Her pulse hammers in her ears. The world beyond, and the world inside, both suddenly alien and full of strangers.

Night carves Lucien's penthouse into sharp panels of shadow and blue. Glass walls look out onto a city that never really sleeps, fluorescent veins pulsing far below, but behind him, only the faint hum of machinery keeps vigil. Lucien moves through the dimness to his private study, fingertips brushing the smooth metal of the door, the echo of Mariel's trembling voice still clinging to his senses. Alone, he doesn't bother with lights—only the bank of encrypted monitors flickering to life, casting faint pools of green and silver up his forearms.

He sets the blackmail letter beside the keyboard, the paper catching a slant of city glow. The screens fill with surveillance mosaics—corridors of Mariel's laboratory in sterile blue, empty except for the occasional ghost of a lab coat or blink of a security badge. Lucien's hand hovers over the controls, knuckles white against the glass, and he forces himself to watch every moment. He knows where betrayal hides: in the obvious, yes, but more often in the soft edges, the split-second glances, things that would drown in noise if not for relentless scrutiny.

The rhythm is ritual, branded into muscle memory from old wounds. He remembers a former protégé, loyal until the moment he slipped a virus into Lucien's own system—how the trust had curdled in less than a heartbeat, how months rebuilding security had felt like living inside a razored shell. He remembers a different midnight, when a breach at his hospital network unraveled while he was home, hands curled around a piano key when his phone screamed with warnings. The technician he had mentored, young and eager-eyed, turned out to be the leak. The memory smolders: nothing, nothing is sacred. Not even bonds forged in sweat and promise.

Now, his eyes flick from camera angle to camera angle, searching for the out-of-place: a figure pausing too long at Mariel's office door, a different gait in the muted light, a flicker of nerves in a face that shouldn't have access after hours. Digital signatures scroll past; he pauses over one that shouldn't exist at 2:16 a.m.—a bypass executed with a code only senior staff know. He isolates the timestamp, rewinds. No face, only a gloved hand pressing against a scanner. A cold line creeps down his spine, half anticipation, half adrenaline. Familiar, yet not; so many years sharpening for just this moment.

Lucien minimizes the window, opening Brotherhood communications archives from the same span. Keyword searches overlay patterns into the early morning: Hodges, Pavel, one or two late-shift scientists. He digs deeper, pulling up innocuous staff memos—yet there, nested in the text, are lines of code that shouldn't be present. Invisible unless one is trained for sabotage. The script pings a warning. A slight smile tugs at his lips, joyless and tight. This isn't just a careless blunder. It's orchestration.

He draws a breath, the taste of old betrayal sharp on his tongue. Is the enemy in the city outside, or winding closer to their shared heart? He can feel the familiar ache of suspicion gnawing at him—no amount of caution is ever enough. He wants to trust, but each pixel of evidence summoned to the glass only deepens doubt. No names yet, but the shape of treachery curls through the system like black smoke.

He pockets the letter, locks his systems, and moves to the Brotherhood's secure conference room long before dawn embitters the sky. The space is heavy with implications—stone walls swallowing sound, a long table of polished wood between Lucien and the others. Caius leans forward, shadow carving deep below his eyes; Darius waits with his arms folded, unreadable.

Lucien lays a dossier on the table. He keeps his voice level, precise. "There's been a breach. Not a random glitch—someone altered Mariel's research streams, timed to coincide with the webcast, and embedded covert signals in staff memos. We're dealing with a professional. Someone inside."

Caius's mouth tightens. "Inside? How deep?"

"Deep enough to fake executive clearance. I won't speculate until I have names—not yet. But the risk is real, and if we start pointing fingers too soon, we hand them more power. I need you vigilant. Limit information, restrict even internal channels. No sudden moves. No trust—except here, or as much as you can muster."

He sits, studying the lines of tension that fracture Caius's stoicism. Darius's eyes glint, voice low. "You think it's one of ours?"

"I think the margin for error is over," Lucien answers. "And so is certainty. Look to your own teams. Review clearances, every one. We can't afford nostalgia."

Their silence is thunder. Caius's knuckles fade white, and Darius's gaze slips away, brows pinched with suspicion—yet beneath, Lucien sees something else: the dissolution of an old faith, the first splinter.

When the meeting ends, Lucien waits for their footsteps to fade before slipping the evidence into the hidden wall safe. The room settles into silence once again, darker than before—a silence heavy with the scent of cold stone, a night without trust.

Deep beneath the city's waking pulse, the Brotherhood gathers. The hidden council chamber hums with the silent weight of secrets. Darkness presses in against the dim amber glow of the sconces while the round table, hewn from a single slab of blackened oak, dominates the center. Starlight winks from the fiber optics overhead—echoes of constellations that once symbolized unity, but now flicker like warning beacons.

Caius takes the seat at the table's head, his presence taut as drawn wire. Lucien sits to his left, knuckles pale against the table's edge, the blackmail letter locked somewhere far colder than his sharp gaze. Mariel's hand rests atop Lucien's, fingers tense, a silent plea for steadiness she fears may be slipping away. The others gather, shadows of themselves: Darius, radiating wary calm; Silas, stone-faced, haunted blue eyes tracking each movement; Orion, a live wire poorly sheathed by bravado; their partners scattering around them, watchful, drawn tight.

The silence fractures as Lucien lifts his gaze. "The sabotage wasn't random." His words slice through the air, precise, stripped of comfort. "Mariel's data was altered by someone with high-level access—someone who knows our protocols. This was no accident."

A chill curls through the chamber. Darius's jaw flexes. "My hospital protocols tripped six unauthorized entries this week. The logs came back clean, as if wiped. If they can ghost through medical security, they're not amateurs."

Silas leans forward, voice low as a storm rumbling beneath surface ice. "Or these are the old rivals. Retaliation, not infiltration. Our enemies have waited years to gut our foundations."

Orion's chair screeches against stone. "You sound awfully certain, Silas. Maybe too certain." He fixes Silas with a glare hot enough to warp steel. "You kept quiet last time we were hit. How many secrets are you sitting on now?"

Silas's mouth sets in a line, blood draining from his knuckles where his fists clench. "Watch yourself, Orion. Paranoia is the quickest way to become the enemy you hate."

"Don't talk about trust," Orion spits, "when you're always disappearing when things go wrong. Caius, tell me you aren't blind to this."

Caius's eyes glitter with suppressed fire. "Enough. If we tear into each other, we finish what our enemies started." He turns to Lucien. "Is there proof? An insider?"

Lucien shakes his head, voice tight. "Just patterns. Too many to ignore, too few to name. We can't accuse blindly."

In the margins, Elara's hands form gentle shields around Orion's trembling fists. "This is exactly what they want. We can't let suspicion cut deeper than any outside knife." She scans the group, her voice calm with tempered resolve.

Lila leans closer to Darius, her touch light but intent. "We know each other. Don't let this spread further. We survived worse than this—together."

But the air sharpens, tempers sparking off old scars. "Survived for what?" Orion snaps. "To watch everything fracture now?"

Even Mariel's steady poise falters. Her eyes dart from Lucien to the walls, as if she could decipher a solution hidden in polished stone. "We're not finished. We can't be. This—" she gestures, shaking "—is what they're after. Our fear."

Her heart races loud in her own ears, beats echoing the tension threading through Lucien's spine. Under the table, Lucien's own grip only tightens. Even here, with Mariel beside him, every sideways glance between the Brotherhood burns with the memory of betrayal: old scars reopening, doubts spreading like infection. The partners—normally anchors—seem adrift, orbiting their billionaires but unable to steady them.

Caius rises, his voice coiled and iron-hard. "We need surveillance. On everything. Limit contact outside this room. No more trust without proof." His glance is more decree than suggestion.

A cold silence blankets the chamber. Seraphina stands, shoulders straight as a drawn blade. "Enough." The word lands like a crack across stone. "We either contain this, or we lose more than reputations—we lose each other."

Everyone hesitates. The cost of mistrust tangles the air, heavy as winter fog.

One by one, resigned nods take the place of understanding. The plan forms, but it trembles, every compromise another fracture under pressure. Consensus achieved, yet each member's compliance is brittle—a mask over uncertainty.

When the council's doors open and lamplight spills into the corridor, the couples scatter, some clutching hands, others walking apart, voices hushed and raw. The starlit chamber remains, thick with a chill they cannot shake, as if the stone itself doubts they will survive what's coming.

Whispers in the Hospital

The hospital corridor, always awake even before dawn, breathes with controlled urgency. Lights cast soft halos through tall arched windows, catching in columns of dust above the stone-gray floors. Darius's shoes move with brisk certainty, his white coat fluttering, but his mind lags behind—still turning over last night's chaos. In the ICU wing, three critical care monitors pulse red with error screens, electronic alarms sounding off—bright, sharp notes that cut through the muted hush of early morning. Nurses murmur in tense voices behind glass, improvising with analog charts where machines have failed them. In surgery, two procedures have been pushed back, scrub teams left idling as the sterilized trays they need can't be found. The smell in the halls is a mix of disinfectant and damp earth, a storm spent outside but not forgotten inside the walls.

Darius's hands clench and release reflexively. Every misfire echoes as both a personal affront and a collective danger. He checks the monitors himself, hoping for an easy fix—loose cables, a blown fuse. Nothing. The flaws run deeper: invisible, calculated. He moves toward his office, his mind already dividing the world into sectors—ICU, surgical, admin—mapping out vulnerabilities the way a chess player charts a board after a clandestine move in the dark. It's a careful balancing act, maintaining the façade of control while dread gnaws beneath his disciplined surface.

Inside his office, the air is less sanitized, layered instead with the warm, bitter tang of yesterday's coffee. Darius is bent over incident reports, each page thick with numbers and complaints—words he's grown to recognize as the handwriting of fear. His jaw aches from tension. The door opens softly, and Lila enters with silent grace. She places a steaming ceramic mug beside his hand, her fingers brushing his sleeve just long enough to be felt but not noticed by anyone passing in the hall. Lila's presence draws warmth into the sterile light of the room; it's the scent of coffee and her faint perfume—a breath of citrus and something floral, grounding him.

He doesn't look up, but she senses the edge in his stillness. Through the glass, nurses hover, one knocking—a stack of new problems in her arms. Darius nods at Lila, and she smiles slightly, a private gesture reserved for these solitudes. On the other side of the door, voices spill like water over stone—staff needing guidance, patients needing hope. Lila murmurs reassurances: "Five minutes. He'll be there when he can." She closes the door, and the world narrows, for a moment, to just them.

Darius leans back, his hand absently tracing the scar on his forearm—a physical memory of another crisis, another betrayal. Lila slides into the seat across from him, her eyes kind but watchful. She waits, the way she always does, for him to give voice to the ghosts crowding his mind.

"I'm losing the thread, Lila," Darius admits, his voice rougher than he wants. "Medication errors have tripled this week. Last night, someone almost gave a child the wrong dosage. It wasn't just rushed—it was... deliberate. Or someone wants it to seem that way."

Lila nods, worry flickering in her hazel eyes. "One of the night nurses found files—personnel records—scattered across the administrative lounge before morning. Just dumped, as if someone ransacked the place and wanted us to know they were there." Her fingers wrap around her mug, and she slips him a folded note, jotted down with times and names. "If they're trying to rattle us, it's working. People are on edge."

He pushes a stack of reports aside, rising to stand at the broad window. Outside, ivy shimmers with rainwater, the city emerging gold and green in the tentative dawn. His reflection in the glass looks older, harsher.

"I can't delegate this," he says softly, as if admitting a dangerous secret. "If I let it slip—if someone gets hurt—every bit of trust I've built, every life weighed on this place, it's mine. The Brotherhood, this hospital, all of it. No more hiding behind procedures. I need to see for myself who's moving the pieces."

Lila joins him by the window, her presence a gentle pressure at his side. "Not alone," she says quietly. "You've taught me that strength comes from not bearing the storm yourself, Darius. We'll see it through. Together."

Another knock, then the sudden shrill rise of a corridor alarm—a code called overhead. The distant clatter of running steps. Darius feels the ground slip toward chaos, but Lila's hand finds his, fingers tight—a silent anchor in the tumult.

She looks up at him—eyes fierce, her voice low. "Whatever's coming, we do this as one. Let them try to break us."

And in the next breath, another morning begins its slow collapse.

The hands of the antique clock in Darius's office tremble toward noon as stray sunlight sifts through tall windows, dust motes swirling in the beam like uneasy spirits. The air inside is tinged with the subtle scent of disinfectant, layered over the tang of coffee and the faint metal of machinery. There's quiet here, but not calm—a hush braced before the next upheaval.

Darius sets his worn leather bag at the edge of his vast ebony desk. He glances across papers in disarray, reports half-annotated, red ink raked over errors that breed like mold. In the center of the desk sits an envelope the color of bone, no mark or flourish betraying its origin. He reaches for it, pulse speeding up. Paper crackles—a thin, sharp, unnatural sound. He slides a finger under the flap, unfolding the single sheet inside.

"Stop digging or lose everything," the message declares—faceless, typed, carrying that ugly sting that presses into his spine. No signature, just the faint ghost of toner that's already smudged against his thumb.

He presses the intercom. "Dina, did you see who left something on my desk?" His voice claws for control.

The reception nurse's reply is muffled and apologetic. "No, Dr. Vartan. I've only just come on shift. I asked around—no one saw anyone go in."

He swallows, tasting dread on his tongue—dry as old glass. Shadows flicker along the corridor beyond, distorted by the sweep of passing scrubs.

Lila treads softly down the long, waxed hallway, clutching her ID badge and a ring of keys. Her shoes barely whisper over the tile. She ducks into the records room where, beneath the buzz of fluorescent light, the smell of aging paper and ink thickens the air. She moves straight to the locked cabinet, unlocking it with practiced fingers. As she gathers the files—names, numbers, histories binding lives together—her fingers close over something unexpected wedged between the folders.

She draws out a note. The paper is colder than her skin; the message is colder still:

"Those closest will suffer next."

Her breath stutters. The letters are pressed with the same cheap, mechanical precision as Darius's message. She glances behind her, heart pounding—a claustrophobic chill seeps into her bones, as if the records room's closely packed shelves have leaned in, eager to eavesdrop.

Her hands shake, but only a little. Lila pockets the note and clips the files shut, forcing calm into her limbs as she heads for the makeshift sanctuary they'd agreed upon after the last sabotage—a medication storage room, sealed and soundproof.

Inside, the room is dim and bitter-cold, metal shelves lined with sealed vials and the faint scent of isopropyl and latex. Darius stands with his back to the door, shoulders hunched. He turns when Lila enters, reading what's written in her eyes before he says a word.

"They're not just after the hospital," Darius murmurs, his voice slashed by quiet fury. "I found this." He taps the desk with the envelope. "They're inside, Lila. They know my schedule. Maybe ours."

She nods and holds up her own scrap of threat. "I found this in the personnel cabinet. Same hand, different promise."

A charged silence swells between them, heavy as thunder building in distant hills. Darius scans the hard lines of her face—a lifeline, a mirror to his fear—but it's trust that courses between them now, deeper than the wounds bureaucracy leaves. They move instinctively closer, as if proximity itself offers a shield no badge or protocol can forge.

"They're watching us." His hands ball into fists, old scars whitening anew. "I won't let them make you a target. Or anyone else."

Lila leans in, her voice low. "We do this together. That's what scares them. They want to split us, isolate us. But we're not giving them the chance."

A thin smirk tugs at his mouth. "Old tricks, eh?"

She almost smiles. "Let's prove we're not so easy."

Darius fishes his phone out, dialing the head of security with clipped urgency. "Full internal sweep. Tighten monitoring on all admin zones. Lock down new digital security—tonight. Copy that? Good."

He ends the call. The gravity of her gaze weighs on him—unflinching, defiant.

"We don't talk to anyone about the threats except each other," Lila whispers. "Not until we're sure who's listening. Not a word."

He lowers his voice to match hers, a promise pressed into shadow. "No one breaks our circle. Not this time."

They slip into the hallway, light warping across their footsteps, the weight of unspoken history pressing around them. Murmurs drift from a nurse hunched at the far end, worry poisoning the air. The rumors spread like infection—quiet, lethal.

Darius glances sideways at Lila. Their fear sharpens into something resolute, forged in the hush of hidden corners. No matter how deep the hospital's cracks run, together their resolve carves a path through the dark—one step at a time, even as the world listens from the shadows.

Evening settles over the hospital, pale sunlight drained into quiet green corridors stained with the scent of antiseptic and tired hope. The staff break room is half-lit and hushed, its round table pocked by old coffee stains and silent tension. Darius steps inside first, his posture stiff, scanning for shadows clinging beneath the cabinetry. Lila moves behind him, her footfalls feather-quiet. She closes the door, her hand lingering on the knob as the chief of nursing, facilities manager, and head of security settle into mismatched chairs. The clock on the wall ticks out seconds that taste of old anxiety.

Darius sweeps the room with a gaze honed by years of adversaries that wore familiar faces. "Has anyone noticed locked doors left open? Anyone accessing the ICU after hours?" he asks, each syllable clipped, authority wrapped in velvet. His fingers drum once on the chipped wood.

The chief of nursing, a tired woman with worry woven deep into her skin, glances at her ledger. "There was a badge swipe at midnight last night by someone on paternity leave. I thought it was just a systems error." The facilities manager, eyes darting, admits a tool cart inventory came up short at dawn. The head of security pulls at his collar, recalling a flicker of movement on a camera feed—just a shadow, swept away before he could focus.

Lila leans forward, her warmth carefully measured. "Patterns change when someone's hiding. If you think of anything—someone avoiding eye contact, making excuses to linger—it matters." Her voice is quiet, but gets under the skin like a gentle current. She scribbles names, times, and inconsistencies, mapping uncertainty into columns. Darius's focus never leaves their faces; he weighs every hesitation, the way one man scratches his ear and the next flips his badge restlessly.

Old lessons gnaw at him. Trust too easily, and the wolf dons the sheep's coat.

In the operations control room, the hum of hard drives mutes their steps. Lila sits at the terminal, her fingers poised above the keys. Blue light pools under her cheekbones. Darius stands behind her, folding his arms, jaw tense. On the screen, digital logbooks multiply. Lila pulls up access records. Codes and names flicker past.

"There," she murmurs. "Pharmacy. Three fifteen AM." She taps the entry. "Badge: R. Sullivan. But he wasn't on shift—his wife just had a baby."

Darius narrows his eyes. "Someone cloned his access. Or borrowed it." He feels the old ache flare behind his eyes: the memory of the first man he'd trusted, back in the early Brotherhood days, who had handed his fate to rivals for the promise of an empire. Betrayal wears many masks, but always leaves the same cold behind.

"Pull up cameras." His voice slices into the low whirr of machines.

Darius and Lila squint at grainy footage. A figure, hunched in a staff jacket, slips through the swing doors. The body language is all wrong. Confident, almost impatient—a wolf accustomed to moving unseen.

In the hollow hush of an empty administrative office, filing cabinets and an ancient coffee machine keep silent watch. Darius sits, sleeves rolled, a stack of rosters and logbooks arrayed in front of him like a battlefield. Lila perches beside him, ink staining her fingers as she cross-references forms, her brow furrowed in concentration.

"Inventory sheet signatures for morphine," Darius mutters, tracing with one blunt fingertip, "should match Dr. Patel's hand. This looped 'P'—it's off. Compare it with the old ones." Lila thumbs through the files, tension drawing her mouth tight. She pulls a second form free, flattening the paper against the table. The handwriting is mimicked, but sloppy—rushed, emboldened by adrenaline or arrogance.

Dialogue block:

"This isn't just someone taking advantage, is it?" Lila asks, her voice hushed. "They're deep. They know exactly who's on, which doors to use. They're not guessing."

Darius shakes his head, bitterness curling his words. "You don't mimic a signature unless you're planning for weeks. This isn't mischief. It's sabotage."

Lila glances at him, something mournful passing over her face. "Who would do this to a place like this? You've always looked after them—"

He cuts in, his voice suddenly raw. "All the more reason. That's why they picked us." He folds the paper, his hands trembling. "I've seen it before, Lila. People you count on, people who call you brother... They're the ones who know where to cut deepest."

She covers his hand before he can pull away—a silent benediction.

Darius leans over the desk, the air thick with the ghosts of old deceptions and new betrayals.

Dialogue block:

"Whoever's behind this, they're inside. Someone with keys to doors and hearts." His whisper is jagged. "If we move openly, we scare them deeper into the walls. We do this quietly. Together."

Lila's gaze is steady. "We won't let fear make us reckless. We'll watch, listen, and question everything. I trust you. We're not alone, no matter how much it feels like we are."

A quiet understanding passes between them. They gather the forged documents, locking them away in a steel case—the sound is sharp as the day's last hope snapping shut. The office is dim as they step out, their feet echoing along polished stone, night flooding the hallways with new uncertainties.

Storm at the Gates

Orion's penthouse glows with the first shimmer of evening, city lights flickering to life beyond the high glass. The hush is fractured when his phone vibrates—three curt pulses, nothing familiar in the ID. He steps into the living room, its shadows stretched wide across plush rugs and leather. He unlocks the message with a thumb that can't hold steady.

She's not safe. Tonight. You already failed her once. This time, you won't get another chance.

The world shrinks to that handful of words—cold, detached, final. Orion can feel the blood drain from his face, though his cheeks still burn. His hands begin to shake so badly that the phone nearly slips from his grip. In his chest, his heartbeat skitters, then slams, like a fist hammer falling again and again on old scars.

He knows this flavor of fear—a volatile mix of guilt and memory, the acid taste of almost losing Nova before. The memory claws up from the dark corners of his mind: pain, blue hospital sheets, the way her name sounded broken in his throat. Orion's lungs can't pull enough air. His anger—sharp and blinding—rises to barricade the terror before it swallows him. It's the only way he knows to stay upright.

Without thinking, he strides across the expanse of his living room. The glare of the city shifts on glass shelves and polished wood. He grabs a crystal tumbler from the bar and hurls it, glass arcing through yellow light to explode against the black stone fireplace. Shards scatter across the marble. A distant dog barks at the echo.

"Where the hell were you?" His voice ricochets through the space, directed at a security chief whose face pales in the doorway. "Why am I finding out like this? Who's on patrol right now? Double it. I want every approach swept. Are you all asleep up here?"

The chief begins to answer, but Orion's words chop through—barked commands, restless and edged. The staff scurry and disappear like shadows retracting from sunlight. Orion is left in a room that still hums with adrenaline and the faint, metallic tang of fear.

He paces—steps relentless, hands balled at his sides, breath tight. The view outside—all glass, all vulnerability—amplifies the sensation of being exposed, watched, never truly secure. He can't remember the last moment Nova was truly safe.

The elevator hums, and Elara steps into the charged hush. She doesn't flinch at the broken glass or at Orion, who's become a ticking storm. Her gaze finds him—unwavering, patient, concerned. She crosses the space and reaches for his arm, slow and sure.

"Orion." Her voice is low, warm, but carries steel beneath it. "You have to stop picking yourself apart. Blame doesn't protect Nova. Focus does."

Her hand is gentle on his skin, grounding, but Orion recoils as if her touch were flame. He shrugs from her grasp, a wounded animal refusing help, and paces near the windows, city glare drawing hard lines across his jaw. The tension in his muscles is visible, his body a map of battles lost and fought. He wants to keep her at a distance, wants to keep all of them safe by keeping himself dangerous—untouchable.

Elara moves deliberately, circling to cut off his frantic track. She stands before him, spine straight, chin lifted. The fading sky holds a molten edge behind her, painted with desperate color.

"You can't do this alone," she says. The words aren't a plea—they are iron, slow and measured. "And I'm not letting you drown in this. Not tonight. Not ever. We face what's coming together. No matter how dark it gets, Orion, I'm not walking away. Neither are you."

For a moment, he can only stare at her, caught between resistance and release. His throat works. The city flickers behind them—cold indifference outside, warmth struggling inside.

He wants to snap, wants to argue, but the fight's leached out. Instead, his shoulders slump, the storm collapsing inward.

She reaches for his hand again, and this time he lets her take it. Her fingers are smaller, steady, cool where his are fevered. She squeezes, gentle but unyielding.

"I promise," she whispers, her voice threaded with something fierce, "I'm here. We face this. Nova's not alone. You're not alone."

Orion's chest rises and falls, shuddering out some of the poison, if not the dread. The anger, the fear, the need to control—they go nowhere, but are no longer the only things in the room.

Night presses up against the glass, the apartment filling with dusk. Elara stands beside him as the city below buzzes on, oblivious. Above it all, they are two silhouettes locked together in the fading light, balancing between despair and the fragile tether of hope. Orion nods, silent, as if the motion itself is a surrender—a beginning.

Orion sits buried in the hush of his private study, the city's bruised glow splintering through the wall of glass behind him. High above the restless streets, his sanctuary feels more like a cage tonight. He doesn't switch on the lights. Darkness soothes the rawness clawing inside his chest, concealing the tension throbbing in his hands as he presses them together. The penthouse, usually a fortress, has taken on a brittle silence—only the faint thud of security boots in the corridor reminds him the outside world persists in its relentless threat. He shuts his eyes, leans forward into the inky air, and wills his heartbeat to calm. He fails.

He barely registers the tentative knock at first. Elara's voice follows—a soft call, muffled by the heavy door. "Orion? Please, can we talk?"

A current of stubborn heat curls in his gut. If he stays silent, maybe she'll retreat, let him hold the weight as he has before. But the door, the shield he wants, is not enough. He hears the click a moment later: the latch, then Elara, breathing through nerves as she steps inside. Her silhouette shimmers at the threshold—a ghost lit by neon blue city light, shoulders set in defiance of her own fear.

"I need to know why you keep shutting me out." Her voice has a crack in it, jagged with exhaustion and barely controlled pain. She doesn't move closer, arms folded, fingers pressing crescents into her biceps. "You don't get to do this alone, not when we're both in danger." She waits, her breath uneven, willing him to bridge this impossible gulf.

Orion jerks upright, the desk chair grating across the wooden floor. For an instant, his shadow leaps behind him—darker, bigger, a demon gnashing at the boundaries between fury and terror. "You don't understand," he spits, every word sharp as shattered glass. "If anything happens to Nova, to you, it's on me. Not you, Elara. Me. I have to be the one to fix this." His voice cracks, fingers curling tight around the slick edge of his desk, desperate for something solid.

Elara stiffens. She's trembling now, but her chin lifts, gaze blistering through the gloom. "That's not how this works—god, Orion, you think you're alone in this? I can't help you if you push me out every time you're scared. I can't stand by and watch you destroy yourself because you'd rather drown than let me throw you a rope."

"You want to talk about drowning?" His breath quickens, bitterness flaring. "Every time you look at me like I'm some ticking bomb, waiting for me to do something reckless, to fail—don't think I don't see it. I can't—" The words catch. He slams his palm against the desk, rattling the pens and picture frames.

And there it is—every unsaid thing between them, pulsing hot and electric. The risk, the guilt, all the impossible trust that's kept them standing while everything else crumbles.

"How do you think it feels?" Elara's voice is a whip, but the tears threading down her cheek reflect glass and salt in the city glow. "You lock me out, and I'm supposed to what? Pretend I don't care if you tear yourself apart? Pretend Nova isn't part of both of us? I'm done being shut out. We fight together or we break, Orion. You don't get to pick."

Orion stares at her, jaw set, but the fight goes out of his shoulders. Silence smothers the room—a silence thick with everything neither of them dared to say. The view outside flickers: a police siren painting crimson ghost shapes over Elara's hair, the city alive and cruel, so close and so utterly unreachable.

He turns from her, arms braced on the desk, his breath fogging the glass. The muscles in his forearms twitch, body wound like a spring, yet suddenly useless. He wants to smash something, shake off the dread coiling around his spine, scream the world down—but he can't. Not at her.

He used to believe loving someone meant sheltering them from storms, bottling the lightning inside so only his soul burned. He's failed before. If Nova is lost, it will be his undoing. What good is his rage, his strength, if all he does is carve chasms between himself and the few left who anchor him to hope?

He thinks of past nights—some full of urgent touches and whispered promises, others ruptured by the aftermath of danger, Elara coaxing him back from the edge. Her patience: an anchor, a mirror, a challenge. Their love, both armor and wound.

Elara remains, arms taut, hair falling loose as if she's just come in from a storm. The sliver of hallway light casts gold on the sharp angles of her face, making her look at once implacable and breakable. She doesn't leave. She waits, breath ragged, eyes never straying from him, as if sheer will might keep him from drifting further away.

Behind her, the penthouse seems to hold its breath, listening. The friction between them is no longer just anger or fear, but longing buried beneath. Outside, the city sprawls in indifferent constellations. Within these walls, only the fragile hush of an uneasy truce settles, as Elara stands fast, refusing to move.

Orion sits hunched at the edge of the bed, his fingers pressed hard into his scalp, blocking out the cold gleam of the city lights that seep through the picture window. Elara is at the closet, her movements measured and quiet. The soft hiss of zippers, the muted thump of fabric filling a bag—they echo in the hollowed silence between them. Outside, the city seems to crouch, watchful and indifferent, its neon veins pulsing far below the glass, as if nothing has changed. But a chill has claimed the room. Their last words, bitter and ragged, still curl in the air.

The scent of Elara's perfume, subtle and floral, is jarring against the sharp tang of Orion's fear. She slips her charger into the side pouch—calm, practical, a stark counterweight to Orion's tension. He lets his hands fall, staring at the lines etched across his palms as if he could read the answer there.

"We can't stay," he says, his voice thick and low, eyes fixed on the floor. Admitting defeat tastes metallic, like blood in his mouth. She looks over, her eyes soft but unyielding, and nods. No triumph, just relief blurred at the edges with exhaustion.

Minutes later, the penthouse's private lift opens into a shadowy corridor. Two silent Brotherhood operatives—shadows in dark coats—guide them toward the rear exit. Their footsteps merge with the purr of distant engines. Behind them, the penthouse looms: a glass fortress, now nothing but a beacon to anyone watching.

Out on the street, the limo is nondescript, its tinted windows swallowing the world. Orion slides into the back seat, Elara beside him—her hand finds his, not for reassurance but for reality. The journey through the city is ghostly. Skyscrapers bleed light into fog; red stoplights flash on empty intersections like warning hearts. Neither speaks. Their world has condensed to this narrow band of leather and steel, moving them further from the life they built, closer to something unknowable in the dark.

Soon the city gives way to undulating hills, black silhouettes against a bruised night sky. Pines gather at the roadside, needles shivering in the wind. At last, they climb the gravel drive of the safe house, headlights flitting across a small porch and shuttered windows. Inside, the air smells of wood smoke, unfamiliar detergent, and unfamiliar safety.

The Brotherhood's people have ensured the windows are armored, the alarm system new, its soft digital whir almost lost beneath the hush of the forest.

Orion's hands tremble as he tests locks and cameras, stalking the perimeter like a wolf. Elara moves to the kitchen, her steadiness quieting the jitter of old pipes and unfamiliar silence. She fills a battered kettle and sets it to boil. The scent of green tea unfurls, faint but grounding. He joins her at the table—a scarred pine rectangle warmed by a solitary lamp. Between them: a tablet playing silent security footage, a paper map, and two empty mugs.

"You thinking it's someone inside?" Elara asks, her voice softer than usual, but with that edge of steel he's come to rely upon.

"Might be." He stares at the ghostly shapes flickering on-screen. "Could be anyone—someone we missed. Someone who's smarter or closer than we want to believe."

"But what do they want, Orion? The Brotherhood, power—Nova herself?"

He shrugs, a bitter laugh curling in his throat. "Could just be chaos. Could be revenge for something I did before. Doesn't matter—I let it happen. I keep thinking if I'd seen it sooner—"

"Stop," she says, sliding the map away. "No more of that."

His chest tightens. In the wood-paneled stillness, fear spreads inside him—thick, black, choking. He sees Nova's face, pale and vulnerable, every time he closes his eyes. How many times now has he nearly lost everything because of the pitch in his blood, the way he careens for the threat head-on, never stopping to count the cost? Maybe every step he's taken carries its own shadow.

Elara's hand closes gently over his, grounding him to this moment—her thumb stroking the veins on his wrist. "We can't chase every nightmare. But we can face what's next. Together. If the Brotherhood cracks, I won't let you break with it."

He wants to protest. Instead, the energy drains from him like a slow leak. What if he can't keep her—keep Nova—safe? What if all his violence, loyalty, and love were only ever different names for fear?

They slip onto the balcony, where the hush of trees rises through damp air. The forest stirs, countless leaves brushing each other like secrets. Elara leans against him, her arm curling around his waist. For a moment, the tension ebbs. He can almost pretend, here, beneath the startled sweep of stars, that peace is possible.

He breathes her in—tea, pine, the hint of her hair—and finds enough words.

"I'm scared, Elara. Angry, sure, but mostly scared. Sometimes I think there's no end to it—the threats, the darkness. I look at Nova and wonder if peace is something people like us can ever earn."

"You don't earn it," Elara whispers. "You build it. Even out of ruins." She lifts his hand to her heart. "We fight together, Orion. Not apart."

He presses a kiss to her forehead, lips lingering in the warmth of her skin as dawn burns the horizon pale. They stand side by side as new light crawls over the trees, hope coiling between dread and love, bracing for whatever storm the coming day will deliver.

Roses and Ashes

Shadows coil across the penthouse office, stretching long and thin over broken marble slabs. Silas moves restlessly in their wake, the crisp sound of his Italian shoes echoing against scarred stone and fractured glass. In his hand, a tablet reveals the ruins of his kingdom—a pulse of red alerts and scrolling lines of encrypted failure: servers breached at 2:13 a.m., vital commodities rerouted from Monaco to nowhere, media partners issuing retractions with forked tongues. Each new entry is a splinter to the nerves; the digital chaos flickers against his face, casting hard angles in the low light. The air here is cold, sharper for the violence that has passed—beneath it all, faint ozone, the acrid memory of burnt circuitry and panic.

He glances up. The penthouse windows expose a city battered and flecked with light, the skyline jagged and bruised where the last attack sent shards raining down on the streets below. Across the office, the corporate tower's once-perfect order now thrums with alarmed vulnerability. Silas closes his eyes for just a breath, weighing the thin line between fury and fatigue, then taps the screen to summon his lieutenants.

Minutes later, the conference table is a stark rectangle of glass and chrome, perched before the vast night. His advisors—Carter, Lorente, and Marlow—arrive with wary eyes and tense collars. Silas stands, not sitting, forcing his unease into authority. He projects tonight's digital carnage onto the ceiling, the images swimming above them in red script and shadowed overlays.

"We lost secured vendor access at three nodes within the last hour. Payment redundancies held, but it was close. Media control is compromised. Leak vectors are clear—here, here, and here." His voice remains steady, clipped yet precise. "I want full forensic sweeps, prioritized on the upstream intrusion logs. Expect that supply will be hit again. Do not speak of this outside this room."

They fire questions: "Is this the same adversary from last quarter?" "Any chance we've got a whistleblower?" "Are legal teams briefed?"

Silas locks eyes with each in turn, nodding where necessary, cutting off flights of speculation with a motion sharp as a blade. He omits mention of the midnight messages addressed not to him, but to Hana. Her name never crosses his lips. For them, it's data and strategy, risk and containment—the personal stakes remain locked somewhere behind his ribcage, out of reach. The meeting ends with clipped affirmations, his lieutenants departing into the penthouse's flickering gloom.

A quiet moment. In the adjacent lounge, Hana sits, backlit by the bruised, glowing city. Streetlights glimmer through a webwork of broken glass—each reflection casts her in fractured gold and violet. She watches the city, spine straight, hands folded on her lap, outwardly serene. But Silas knows her tension, senses it in the way her thumb rubs the faded scar at her wrist.

He crosses the threshold, his voice measured. "You should clear your schedule tomorrow. Stay close to Marlow and staff you trust." His words are sanded smooth, a practiced calm, concern nestling beneath. "Let Carter handle the travel arrangements. I don't want you unescorted until the situation stabilizes."

Hana tilts her head, eyes meeting his—a quiet challenge in their depths, a question she won't yet voice. She rises, lips parting. "That bad?"

"It's manageable," he says, already retreating toward tasks he can control. "Just a precaution." Unspoken: how thin that word feels tonight, how little it covers.

Silas returns to his desk, the glow of the monitor blue-white on his hands. He types out coded instructions to his private security detail—double the watches, restrict all access, scan comm logs for anomalies. The system pings softly as he reroutes proprietary data to an offline vault, digital assets slipping into darkness, unreachable. He takes a slow breath, fighting the shake in his limbs, willing his reflection in the glass to remain unreadable.

His mind races—how close did the breach come? How many enemies hide behind familiar passwords and polite emails? He imagines rooms like his, somewhere out there, with men in borrowed loyalties coordinating his ruin.

Sometimes he wonders if this is what real power feels like: the world narrowing around him, each act a calculation, each word a mask. There's comfort in action—for now—but each step piles on more dread. The need to protect Hana claws at him raw, threatening the composure that keeps his empire breathing.

He thinks of his father's old cautions, the iron voice of legacy: Trust is a liability. Love is a fissure. Yet every protective command he issues for Hana is laced with guilt, as if warning her were an arrow pointed back at himself. He wonders how much longer he can keep the two halves separate—the merciless executive and the man who aches at the thought of losing her to the shadows bleeding into their world.

After the last protocol blinks green, Silas stands, crossing to the battered window. The city's arteries pulse below—serpentine, unbroken, indifferent to his fear. In the spiderwebbed glass, his reflection stands divided: one part the phantom king clutching at a crumbling throne, the other simply a man, pulse hammering wildly under his wrist, watching for dawn that may not come.

Sapphire and white lights flicker across the marble floors of the gala ballroom, splintering into fractured rainbows beneath the weighty gaze of a crystal chandelier. Hana moves through the current of finely dressed guests, her presence like a soft ripple against the surge: understated black silk, delicate earrings, eyes bright above a measured smile. The scent of gardenias trails behind her, nearly smothered by the bite of dry champagne and the brine of chilled oysters offered on mirrored platters. A string quartet unwinds something silvery in the background, though the melody stutters against the low static of tense conversation.

She nods at a donor's joke, notices her own reflection—composed, inscrutable—gliding in the shine of a mirrored pedestal. Security personnel dot the perimeter in midnight suits. Everything feels too orchestrated, too sharp. Hana registers the strangers at the auction table, a man and a woman—neither part of the social ecology here, eyes darting slick from crowd to clipboard and back to her. Their attention hovers, sticky as the condensation beading down her untouched glass of wine.

A tremor blooms beneath Hana's ribs, soured by memory and the tang of threat. Silas's warnings echo in her mind, but she presses a smile into place. Tonight, she is clarity itself.

She slips away with practiced grace, murmuring an apology about a call from Seoul, letting her shadow fall into the gilt restroom. A whisper of linen against tile, a hush of perfume and muted laughter from outside. Hana perches by the marble sink, thumbs flicking over her phone, wrists steady.

"Can you pull the last twenty minutes on the main auction?" she types to Silas's IT director, "and background on catering. Three, maybe four unknowns. Discreet, please." Her heart rattles in her chest—there's a strange thrill in this, the control of it, like walking a tightrope with no net but her own resolve. She smooths her hair, checks the lock. Alone, she lets her mouth set into a line, the veneer of poise thinning under the fluorescent lights.

The ballroom's air feels heavier as she returns. People laugh, clinking flutes, oblivious to invisible fault lines splitting the evening open. Hana catches the brief flicker of one stranger's gaze, but she has already begun to move, weaving through the press of bodies toward the exit. The city beyond the glass gifts her a different kind of anonymity—rain on the streets, the distant rush of tires on wet pavement, neon bleeding along the edges of her reflection in the car window.

Home is a high-rise breathing with silence, their kitchen painted by the faint gold of city lights refracted through scattered rain. Hana peels off her earrings, rolling her tension into a ball and tucking it deep as she dials the number of her friend, Mina.

"You up?" Hana asks, her voice soft, edged with urgency. "I need intel. Something's happening—same pattern as the last breaches. Who's behind it?" Her words are measured, precise. She listens to

Mina's reply, piecing fragments together in her mind—a map of dangers converging, a constellation forming just beyond her grasp.

Silas waits in the kitchen, his eyes shadowed by strain. He watches her in silence as she slips off her heels and pours a glass of water with steady hands.

"You left early," he says. The words are soft, but his posture is rigid—shoulders squared, jaw marked with fatigue. The refrigerator hums between them. She sets the glass down, meets his gaze, her own face unyielding.

"I saw men watching me who didn't belong. I had IT pull the tapes. I asked Mina for off-the-books connections. You said I should stay close, but you didn't say why." She folds her arms, her voice flat but vibrating with something electric. "We're past the point of you shielding me by telling half-truths, Silas. If I'm a target, I need full context. All of it. No more decisions behind closed doors."

He narrows his eyes, his lips pressed thin; there's a brief flash of something like hurt. "It's not just business, Hana. There are lines I can't risk crossing—risking you. The threats... they're different this time."

"And you think hiding them keeps me safe?" She steps closer, the distance between them crackling. "That just makes me blind. I'm not your weakness to guard, Silas. I'm your partner. Either I stand beside you or I walk away from a war I can't even see."

His knuckles go white against the marble countertop. "You have no idea what that means. What I carry for you."

"Then give me the weight. Let me see it."

A stretched silence settles. The smog-laden city seems to press up against the glass, impatient for an answer neither of them can yet shape. Fear claws at Hana, but her voice doesn't waver; she's done waiting for rescue on someone else's terms. She sees the ache in

Silas—the effort to lock away terror, the instinct to hold her apart from strife.

At last, he steps forward, rough palms catching her trembling hand. The touch is quiet and deliberate.

He doesn't let go. Not tonight. Not any longer.

Beyond the city's broken reflections, deep underground, the Brotherhood's council chamber breathes with secrets and foreboding. No windows here—just the glinting granite walls that catch every movement, every flick of a wary glance. Silas enters first, Hana beside him, her slim hand tucked through his arm. Their footsteps fall softly on the flagstone as they approach the round table, each high-backed chair bearing the constellation: five stars burned into blackened oak, joined by silvered lines.

The others file in quietly—Caius, Lucien, Darius, Orion, and their partners—a circle half-shadowed, half-lit by the star-studded glow that pulses above, a false sky stitched with hope and warning. Tension clings to the air, prickling skin, sharpening senses. Even beneath this fortress of earth, the danger outside presses inward, a storm on distant shores.

Silas lays a tablet on the table's scarred surface. Dust motes catch the amber light as he speaks, his voice low and even. "The timeline—" His thumb swipes through timestamps and digital trails: server breach, payroll hack, the siphoning of medical supplies. "Whoever's behind this, they're not just after money. They're leaving breadcrumbs. Threats. Some uniquely... personal." His voice nearly breaks, but he's already weighing his words, keeping Hana's name hidden in the lines between facts. Still, when he brings up the threats encrypted with her childhood nickname, every partner in the room goes still.

Caius leans forward, elbows on the etched oak, his eyes flickering with contained fire. "This isn't your fight alone, Silas. My tech team's rerouting the top-end firewall suites tonight. No gaps."

Lucien's pale knuckles rest on a bulging folder. "We've flagged a half-dozen new hires—IT, admin, even a PR intern. I have their backgrounds compiled. I trust no one but us for the next thirty days, minimum." His words are clipped and precise.

Darius's calm surfaces in a softer offer—an email address, a burned phone, a direct line to his hospital's secure network. "Your messages disappear the moment they're read; double authentication, medical-grade encryption."

Orion, always a beat sharper—rage and loyalty stitched together—nods at Silas. "My estate's fallback staff are ex-military. If your tower goes any darker, send her up the hill. My gates are closed to anyone but Brotherhood, no exceptions."

Beside Silas, Hana keeps her posture straight, her jaw set. Her gaze sweeps the table, meeting every partner's eyes, an unspoken plea for solidarity and, beneath it, gratitude edged with steel.

They argue logistics, then silent protocols. Darius suggests a round of daily check-ins; Lucien expands, "Digital and human—never just one." Caius insists on a single, rotating intel officer to avoid a weak link, and Orion demands staggered home addresses for all partners—no one should become a pattern.

And when the talk ebbs, the council votes. Unanimous: No one stands alone now. Each promise passes between them like a live current, pulling the thread tighter, weaving the constellation that began so long ago.

In the chamber's hush, Silas drifts to the edge as the meeting dissolves. Beside him, Hana stays silent. She leans into his side, her head just brushing his shoulder. The starfield above flickers, and for a heartbeat, the hidden weight between them eases. His hand finds hers, rough and cold against her delicate fingers. No words pass—none are needed.

In the chamber's charged gloom, memories gather: five men eight years younger, bruised by defeat or hunger, swearing fidelity beneath this same painted sky. The sigil at the table's center took shape on Silas's own desktop: five stars, a pivot point for everything they sacrificed. What began as leveraged alliances, silent fears, and the blunt force of necessity had, over the years, softened into something relentless and alive—family built not just by profit and power, but by the unbroken promise to shield each other when night closed in.

Yet inside, Silas's nerves are raw and exposed. The urge to hide, to shield Hana from the blast radius, wars with the truth: secrets breed fractures, and fractures are what the enemy counts on. He feels himself balancing on the divide—the man who locks data behind ten passwords, the lover whose arms have started trembling in sleep. Leadership asks for everything, and when the losses tally up, you begin to question not just your tactics, but your heart.

Still, surrounded by these faces—Caius's shrewd intensity, Lucien's haunted focus, Orion and Darius pulling the Brotherhood's line unbroken—Silas tastes something rarer than hope. He clings to it in Hana's quiet presence, in the wordless press of her palm to his.

A voice cracks the quiet. Seraphina, her accent a lilt on the air—"We're all visible now. No more shadows to hide behind. That's our choice, isn't it?"

Caius answers, his voice warm but grave. "We never hid, not truly. Not from each other."

Lila murmurs, "Then we stand together, or not at all."

It is enough. For this hour, beneath this starless earth, unity holds. And as Silas draws Hana close beneath the echo of old oaths and flickering fiber optic skies, fear is, for a moment, outshone by the certainty that none of them will weather the coming storm alone.

The Gathering

Sleek black walls absorb much of the LED spill, rendering the ultramodern conference room a geometric void edged with muted reflections and sharp, shadowed corners. The air's chill hums with sterile sterility, the faintest tang of polished chrome and electronics mixing with the distant trace of bergamot from Caius's coat as he strides in first, Seraphina tight at his side. Their footfalls run silent across graphite tiles. Before settling at the round, blackened oak table, Caius's eyes trace every contour of the ceiling and corners—quick, exacting, each glance a calculated challenge to unseen watchers. His frame remains carved in tension, jaw set, like a general stalking enemy lines. Seraphina unzips her compact case, revealing a nest of jammers and signal detectors; her fingers move quickly, cool as she sweeps a handheld across the comm units embedded in the table—listening, watching, scanning. A breath catches in her chest as she finds nothing—yet nothing lately brings comfort.

Lucien and Mariel's arrival is all soft leather shifting and brisk but measured steps. Lucien pauses at the entry, his crisp suit unruffled, pressing his thumb to the biometric lock; a faint chime and a flare of green. His gaze lingers on the jamb, mouth drawn into a line, as if decoding hidden threats behind innocuous mechanisms. Mariel enters, already reading, blue light rippling across her tablet's glass. She scrolls through spilled threat feeds—numbers and incident alerts stacking beside jagged red flags. She meets Caius's nod with her own careful tilt, a wordless exchange hung with the weight of recent failures. Lucien claims the nearest chair beside her, always angled to keep the door in his periphery.

The room senses new motion—Darius, resolute but haunted, guiding Lila inside. He keeps his coat on as he crosses to the embedded screen controls and calls forth a live wall of security camera feeds: endless loops of sterile hospital corridors and shadowed loading bays flicker into existence above the table. He scans them, jaw twitching as if he's bracing for everything to unravel. Lila moves quietly, her greeting to Seraphina a soft, steady thread that wavers beneath the surface—a little too careful. She squeezes Seraphina's shoulder in a reassurance meant as much for herself. Under the lights, her hands tremble, quickly stilled by a tense exhale.

Doors sigh open again. Orion storms through, shoulders hunched with the storm of twenty sleepless hours in his frame. In his fist, a jagged-edged incident report—he tosses it onto the table where it lands with a dull slap. Elara follows close, her silence a shield, eyes mapping the nervous staccato rhythm of the group. She senses it in the way Lila doesn't release Seraphina's hand, the way Darius's fingers hover over the screen controls long after the feeds stabilize.

Silas's entrance is last and least yielding. He steps in, Hana shadow-silent beside him. His gaze sweeps the room with razor economy, taking attendance and measuring threat in every body. He slips his hand around Hana's as if anchoring them both. Hana shoots Lila a look—brief, gentle, promising solidarity with only the faintest crease at the corners of her eyes.

A hush bleeds through after the last click of the door. Caius's voice cuts through it—low, clipped, the static in it a warning bell. He opens the meeting, fingers drumming the table. "Our empires bleed. Each strike lands with surgical precision—patterns that cut wider, deeper, every week. Industrial sabotage, data breaches, targeted threats. Not random. Not desperate. Whoever's orchestrating this knows every-thing—operations, schedules, even the code buried in our security protocols." His scar creases as he scans the faces arrayed like chess pieces before him.

Lucien's voice, cool and tempered: "The breach at Mariel's facility wasn't brute force. They bypassed airlocked labs, broke our firewalls as if they'd written them. And they ghosted out—no digital footprints, no trace left for us to chase." Mariel pinches the bridge of her nose, her tablet trembling slightly as she scrolls to the relevant incident feed. "Every safeguard has been circumvented. Someone inside, or someone with access to everything."

Darius keys up hospital logs on the wall. "It's the same pat-tern—we're seeing manipulated records, equipment that fails at the worst possible moment, and it's endangering lives. Even someone on my payroll is scared, reluctant to log anything without double-check-ing—trust is evaporating."

Orion leans forward, voice flattened to iron. "At my estate, they tried to cut power to the animal quarter—went straight for Nova. My guards caught movement, but the intruders vanished before anyone could get a real look. The way they moved...it was like they'd lived there before." Elara's hand reaches for his, squeezing gently. "They knew about security rotations. We found marks on a panel only you—or I—could disable. We're being watched from the inside."

Silas speaks, a taut thread unraveling. "Every time I change protocols, the leaks adapt. Threats come for Hana—direct, chilling, quoting things only my closest know." He glances at Hana, her serene mask barely hiding the flicker of fear in her eyes. "My teams are either compromised, or we have a puppet master pulling their strings."

A dialogue block:

"So what do you propose?" Lucien's tone is all hard angles, eyes sharp as frost. "Accuse our own? Tear apart every team from within?"

Darius's reply is measured but underscored by strain. "We'll have to if survival means rooting out rot. But if we pull too hard, we might pull down everything we've built."

Another dialogue block:

Seraphina leans in, fire in her gaze. "If you think I'll sit by while someone in our house betrays us—"

Elara's voice is quiet, but steady. "No one's suggesting we start a witch hunt. But closure means honesty. If we can't trust each other, we're handing them victory already."

A silence thick as storm clouds follows—heavy and unrelenting. Faces flicker in the LED glow, features hardened by sleeplessness, fear, and unspoken doubt. Each couple's eyes linger on the others, weighing memories against new, mounting suspicion. The attacks—they're too precise, too intimate. Coincidence falls away, leaving the stark shape of betrayal.

Caius's hand presses flat to the table, a slow, final gesture that grounds the collective dread. "Whoever's doing this—they know us. Every secret, every blind spot. They're not an outsider. They're one of us."

Lucien's hands move with fluid precision over his keyboard, tapping out commands that echo softly around the ultramodern conference room. The glow from his encrypted laptop flickers, illuminating his features—a mask of careful intent hiding stormier thoughts. On the wall behind him, a digital map blossoms across one black surface, constellations of red, green, and amber points dancing into crisp formation. Each luminous line traces the arc of a breach: systems sliced open in the dark, patterns threading through empires once ironclad.

"We need to deploy every cyber unit at our disposal," Lucien says, voice flat, measured, clipped at the edge. "There are patterns here. Someone's not just throwing darts in the dark. See the timing of these breaches—exactly eleven minutes after shift rotation at Darius's hospital, nineteen seconds after our own digital vault resets." A faint tremor stirs at the corners of his mouth, as though the implications taste bitter.

Darius steps forward, broad shoulders tense beneath his tailored jacket, eyes tracking the shifting vectors onscreen. He stands close enough to smell the ozone tang of recently cycled servers wafting from a hidden air duct. "Insider knowledge," Darius murmurs, more to himself than anyone. He brings up a feed with a gesture—surgical, deliberate—displaying a three-way split of security camera grids, patient log anomalies, and a hospital corridor bathed in spectral light. "We won't beat this with isolated fortresses or old loyalty oaths. I propose a full surveillance mesh. Every facility—hospital, research, and corporate—streams into a single command. We'll cut off leaks before they learn to breathe."

From across the round table, Silas looks up, his blue eyes limpid but unreadable. His words emerge in a whisper, flat and deliberate: "That won't be enough. Our protocols were designed for compartmentalization, not alliance. I want everything integrated—real-time, no delay.

The moment something blips, every entity is alerted. I'll adapt my team's firewalls, bring the network up to parity. If there's a breach, no one faces it alone. Not again."

There's a flicker of tension—one of many, subtle as the air's chill. Caius tracks it, feels his own jaw clench, his heartbeat picking up its riotous drumbeat beneath the starched rigidity of his shirt. Every instinct strains against the urge to pace, to do, to control the chaos bleeding through the seams of their unity. Rivalries are here, unspoken but sharp, flaring in the way Silas's words slice the air, the way Darius's eyes flick—just briefly—to Lucien's hands.

Elara's voice interrupts the undercurrents, steady as dark water. "If we're going to build this, we need more than connected servers. We need a framework—roles, responsibilities, twice-daily check-ins. Defined channels so no one is isolated. If we don't trust the system, it'll fall apart before the first alert goes through." Her gaze finds each person in turn, lingering on Seraphina, Lila, and Hana—a silent signal, forging bridges where suspicion breeds fissures.

Caius lets himself exhale, marking the moment with a nod. He draws himself taller, pushing authority into every word. "Lucien, Darius, Silas—all of you, start building our command hub. Shared eyes, shared alarms. Seraphina, Elara—get evacuation plans in place for everyone our enemy might target." He pauses, catching Mariel and Lila's expectant focus. "You two—tear apart every financial transaction, every digital trail. Find anything that doesn't match our patterns. Twenty-four hours. That's all we have before they move again."

Files change hands in crisp succession—memory sticks, paper folders with crisp edges, encrypted drives that gleam like obsidian in harsh LED light. Fingers brush, knuckles tighten, a stray bead of sweat traces down Lila's wrist as she flicks files over to Mariel. Worried eyes meet, linger, and dart away. Suspicion is here in every movement, every too-brisk exchange. Yet so is something else—a fragile commitment, a vow forged not in comfort but necessity.

No one remarks on the subtle ways alliances form: Orion, restless, glances at Elara for an unspoken calibration before gruffly passing him diagnostic codes. Hana and Lila exchange nods across the table, silent vows etched through shared exhaustion. The taste in the air is artificial, faintly chemical, but beneath it hums something far older—fear, urgency, hope.

"Ready for the signatures." Lucien's tone is low as he pushes his chair back. Caius rolls his biometric ring—heavy, cold—between his fingers, hesitating a fraction too long. The others rise with him, the air charged and expectant.

Dialogue block:

"Elara, do you think the council's ready to trust this system?" Seraphina asks, not bothering to soften the steel in her voice.

Elara's answer is a slow exhale. "Ready or not, it's all we have. If someone falters, the whole thing falls. But I trust each of you more than the shadow outside."

Caius presses his palm to the interface. The scanner's glow turns blood-red, then softens to green. Each of them follows—Lucien's hand steady, Darius's tense, Silas's a ghosting tremor, while the partners lend their signatures with only the faintest pause of dread. The document's holographic seal blossoms in blue light above the table, spinning like a conjured sigil—beautiful, fragile, binding.

Dialogue block:

"You do realize this makes us a single target now," Orion mutters, rubbing the scar on his jaw.

Lucien's reply is dry. "Would you rather stand alone and be picked off one at a time?"

Orion's smile is all wolf. "Didn't say I planned to be easy prey."

Elara's hand gently settles over his, quieting further retort. Around them, no one laughs.

The hush that falls is nearly sacred. As the luminous seal fades, Caius meets each gaze. Trust is thin—almost invisible—but for a moment, in the sterile light, it exists.

The lounge burrows deep into shadow, a sanctuary for secrets that refuse to sleep. Muted lamplight skims across low velvet armchairs and pools with amber glow onto the tension-warped faces of the Brotherhood and their partners. The outside world is quiet—too quiet—but in here, nerves simmer louder than any city siren.

Seraphina's hands trace slow, restless circles across her forearm, over the old scar no one else notices. The urge to speak claws at her throat, fierce as wildfire, but the first word emerges a fractured whisper. " I... Something's wrong," she begins, her voice trembling against the charged hush. "I can't shake it. Every attack—too precise, too close. And I think—" The confession lurches out, raw as a wound. "I think someone inside is betraying us."

The words hang for a beat, heavy, their truth coiling with the scent of stale coffee and the distant tang of cleaning chemicals that never succeed in purging fear from the air. Chairs shift. Leather creaks. Caius sits forward, face cut with hard lines, while Lucien's fingers drum the glass-smooth tabletop, the sound biting into the silence.

Mariel clutches her tablet so tightly her knuckles blanch. It's as if the device might dissolve beneath her grip, taking her anxiety with it. She looks down, her eyes catching the reflected image of her own frown in polished metal. "There's been a leak," she admits, the syllables shaky but determined. "Sensitive research data—weeks now. I thought I had it contained, but..." Her voice thins to nothing, regret leaking between the clipped phrases. "If it's connected... it's my fault they got in so far."

Darius's gaze sharpens, calculations ticking behind his calm exterior, but Lila steps close to Mariel. She touches her arm—a gentle anchor. "It could've happened to any of us," Lila says, but the strain runs like fine cracks beneath her steadiness.

Lila's own doubts gather. She turns to Elara, keeping her voice quiet but urgent. "We're moving fast. Too fast. Should we really be sharing everything? What if all this transparency makes us more vulnerable?"

Elara's response is steady, her eyes finding Lila's in the low light. "We can't close ourselves off now. Secrets are what got us here. If we hide, we feed the enemy's power." Her hand, though, betrays the tiniest tremor—a ripple of nerves she refuses to let rise any higher.

Meanwhile, Hana sits hunched on the far edge of a velvet settee, knees drawn close. She notes the fatigue blurring Silas's watchful stare, the sleepless defeat in the set of his jaw. Around her, tension snakes through the room: Mariel's voice thinning, Lila's whisper pitched on a thread, Elara's poise frayed at the seams. Hana presses her lips together, sensing the exhaustion digging under everyone's skin.

The lounge grows fractured. Whispers sharpen like wires as each couple pulls into their own orbit. Caius leans in toward Seraphina, his voice a low rumble edged with steel. "You think the betrayal runs that deep?"

Seraphina nods, shoulders tight. "It's not just skill. It's knowledge—patterns only someone close could map." Her gaze flickers, seeking reassurance. Caius returns it with the faintest squeeze of her hand, but even he can't mask the shadow that leaps into his eyes.

Mariel hisses softly to Lucien, "I should've come forward sooner. How much damage have I done?"

Lucien's reply is almost inaudible, full of a brittle sort of tenderness. "You did what you thought kept us safe. No one expects perfection, Mariel. Not now."

Across the room, Lila and Elara's debate continues in hushed tones that rise above the pulse of the lamp's low hum.

"If we keep every card close," Lila insists, "paranoia will eat us alive."

"And if we reveal everything," Elara counters, voice flinty, "what's left to defend ourselves? There's a line—we have to see it, or we become just as dangerous as our enemies."

From the shadowed corner, Hana watches the tremor in Elara's hand, the way Silas keeps glancing at the entrance as though the night might send something worse than betrayal through its door. She watches, too, as Mariel bends beneath invisible burdens and Lila's gentle confidence wavers. Words ricochet—accusations unspoken, apologies swallowed. The air thickens with old grievances, the sense of unity buckling beneath the weight of suspicion.

In the early morning hush, the pulse of anxiety hammers through Hana's chest. She draws slow breaths, cool and sharp, as her gaze drifts to the sliver of city lights far beyond the lounge's lone narrow window. Glass streaked with condensation, evidence of the press of bodies and feverish secrets inside.

She sees her reflection—small, solitary—caught between the shimmer of the distant skyline and the brooding dark within. Out there, the night promises nothing except more shadows, more doubt. In here, bonds forged in danger fray at the slightest pull.

Fatigue numbs her, but still, hope flickers—a thin violet flame refusing to bow to suspicion. She lets her forehead rest against the chilled pane, breath fogging the glass, a silent vow echoing in her chest: No matter how deep the wounds go, she must remember the fragile promise of unity, even as darkness claws at the edges.

The First Retaliation

The war room hums with tense energy—polished obsidian surfaces reflecting the constellation of faces clustered around the central table. Walls flicker with projection maps, pulsing live feeds cascading across screens, the room's chill pierced by scents of stone, electrified copper, and cologne. Sealed inside this fortress—Caius's private stronghold—no city noise penetrates, only the subtle clicks of secure locks and the faint, vigilant hiss of the estate's tech-laden heartbeat.

Caius stands at the head of the table, posture rigid—a marble statue come alive beneath the recessed lights. His shadow leans into the glass walls, the scar catching the white shine as if branded with purpose. Seraphina lingers at his side, dark hair brushed behind her shoulders, that old scar on her forearm a barely healed boundary between war and peace. Around them, Lucien's brow furrows as he studies encrypted patterns, Mariel sharp-eyed even as fatigue traces her mouth. Darius fingers a slim folder, Lila's hand steady atop his, and Orion paces, restless as always, but anchored by Elara's calm stare. Silas arrives last, Hana silent at his flank, the pair moving with the wary grace of predators in uncertain territory.

The Brotherhood is no longer a cohort of lords clutching secrets within glass towers. Tonight, for the first time, they stand arrayed for a coordinated attack. The room itself—layered with bio-locks, voice scramblers, and walls tuned to absorb every whisper—serves as both shield and command post. A map on the main screen glows with target sites: hospital, research lab, estate grounds, financial towers, each a chessboard now armed for war. Here and now, the old codes of silent retaliation fall away. Caius's voice slices through the hush, measured and cold as marble.

"We strike at four points. No second chances. Lucien, Mariel—intercept, cut the enemy's channels at the source. Darius, Lila, track the rat in your supply chain—eliminate quiet leaks before they drown us. Orion, Elara, you know your grounds. I want every hired hand with shadowed intent on their knees by sundown. Silas, Hana—trace the money, burn the saboteurs inside your house. No mercy." He leans on the table, gaze pulling each of them to attention. "We turn the hunt. This is the line."

He feels the weight in every silence that follows—a chorus of nods, but also glances traded quickly across the table. It is the gravity of shared purpose, yes, but beneath it: suspicion skirted, the threat of wounds already hidden. Seraphina plants a reassuring hand over his, her fingers cool, a silent pledge. That touch is both fortification and a reminder: strength here costs empathy, and trust is as thin as silk.

Lucien threads the war room's data terminal with silver cables, fingers darting between firewalls and ciphers. Mariel stabilizes the rapid-fire display, cross-referencing badge logs, her voice clipped and focused: "Facility access spike at dawn—unauthorized, by my account. Resetting all clearance." Caius watches the interplay, the clinical precision of old rivals now conjoined by necessity. It is the new order—calculating, relentless, impossible to fracture from the outside, but so easily shaken within.

Far from the glowing screens, Darius and Lila cloak themselves in the sterile air of his hospital annex. Lila stands protectively at his shoulder as they leaf through documents—a shuffled staccato of signatures and timestamps. The sharp scent of antiseptic, the low murmur of hospital machines—these are the background to Darius's realization as he interrupts a staffer at a terminal, voice steel-edged: "Step aside." Lila's eyes meet his, soft but urgent, and together they expose the tampering—an infection rooted not in flesh, but data.

Simultaneously, Orion's estate becomes a storm's eye. He and Elara confront a groundskeeper whose eyes dart, sweat beading along his grimed collar. Orion's temper simmers, words clipped—Elara's voice, calm but razor-sharp, chips at the truths concealed in the man's tight fist. At last, trembling hands drop a phone—encrypted, instructions blinking at the top of the message queue. Elara pockets the evidence, voice low. "You know what happens if you lie." Orion's body vibrates, but he holds.

In Silas's suite, pools of shadow deepen as he pores over shifting numbers, Hana beside him—her presence steady, eyes never leaving his profile. In silence, they chase patterns, her breath warm against the cool air. "Here." Her whisper is almost lost in the drone of city lights, but Silas follows the trail she marks, finding the point where loyalty has bled out through cold accounts. The name they uncover is a grain of grit in the pearl of the Brotherhood—a rogue employee, caught by the net.

Later, they return, each with trophies—data, names, averted disaster. Caius pours whiskey, amber against the blue luminescence. Orion's recounting bubbles with brash relief, Lucien's dry wit surfaces,

Mariel's laughter is edged with exhaustion. They toast quietly, a round of glasses against the void, fear muted in the cavernous room. Yet beneath the celebration, each touch lingers a moment too long, each glance slides away too soon.

Caius surveys the gathering with an unblinking gaze. He sees victories drawn tight as violin strings across tense faces, feels Seraphina's uncertain smile—cracks in the glass, beautiful, dangerous. His pride for their coordinated force is tempered by a chill: every plan can be undone from within. That's the lesson in the shadow behind Seraphina's eyes, the one that will not let him rest. The room grows still, laughter fading to silence as night deepens, and beneath every triumphant heartbeat, suspicion stirs.

Lucien's fingers move swiftly across the illuminated keys, the only sound in his tech hub the low hum of servers and the soft, erratic tapping of his own pulse in his throat. Glass and steel reflect fractured images—his own taut silhouette hunched over a spiderweb of code, Mariel's presence behind him a quiet anchor amid the swirl of digital static. The air's cool, sterile tang is overlaid with the faint, bittersweet scent of coffee she abandoned hours earlier. Shadows flicker on the floor, thrown by the pulse of monitors that bathe the room in blue light, making their faces appear almost uncanny.

Lines of encrypted text shift and jitter, refusing to yield until Lucien breaches the final string—the code collapsing in on itself with a hiss of satisfaction. He freezes as he reads the message: embedded terminology, innocuous at first glance, but the undercurrent is sharp and poisonous. Language borrowed from their own internal protocols. Names—disguised as dates and locations, but unmistakably pointing inward. Double agents, carefully grown like rot beneath a polished surface.

He presses a palm to his mouth, breath hot against his skin, thoughts eddying in that sudden, terrible vacuum: Who? How deep? The very notion of corruption running through his own security team triggers something primal—a warning in the base of his skull, panic barely corralled by cold intellect. He pulls the monitor closer, narrowing in on a sequence—an old friend's ID number, a trusted engineer's initials. He can't trust anyone. Maybe not even—

A gentle hand comes to rest on his arm. He hadn't heard Mariel move, but her touch steadies him, her green eyes searching his, voice pitched low.

"Any progress?"

He exhales—slow, measured—letting his fear slip beneath the surface.

"Depends on your definition."

She looks at him, then, holding his gaze until the moment stretches, taut as wire.

"Don't start withholding from me. Not now. What did you find?"

He hesitates, muscles rigid. For a split second, he wants to lie, shield her, but the pulse of blue code on the screen spills acid into honesty.

"They're not just watching us from the outside. They've burrowed in. We have double agents, Mariel. Embedded in our support staff."

She doesn't flinch, but her fingers curl tighter on his forearm, her mouth a thin line.

"How many?"

"I don't know yet," he admits, his voice barely above a whisper, shame curling in his gut. "Enough that it's no longer a question of loyalty. It's infiltration."

Across the city—a world away in atmosphere—a muted surveillance feed plays in Darius's office, bright screens cutting through the sage dusk. Lila sits beside him, her voice steady but edged with unease as she speeds through footage: empty hallways, the occasional flicker of a badge in the darkness.

"There," she says, pausing the frame. "That's Patel. He's supposed to be on leave."

Darius leans in, reading familiar tension in Lila's jaw. Another badge. Another after midnight. Faces he's trusted for years, stepping into sacred places when the world slept.

"They're all senior. I vouched for each of them. They…"

She covers his hand with hers, the gesture quiet—reminding him they're not alone, even with their pasts yawning beneath their feet.

Silas's downtown office, by contrast, is an aquarium of shadows and half-light, the windows etched with city rain. The only sound is the scrape of paper and the muted click of Hana's pen as she documents every anomaly he finds. His breath is shallow, shoulders tense, as numerical patterns reveal themselves—a hemorrhage of assets, millions siphoned in careful increments. Shell companies with mirrored names, money routed through countries he's never even visited.

"The drain's masked as payroll reconciliation," he murmurs, anger rough in his throat. "But it isn't ours."

Hana places her hand atop his, grounding him. "Whoever did this knew your protocols. Someone close." Her Korean accent gentles the edges of accusation, but he feels the sting—failure isn't just personal; it's existential.

In a secure digital meeting space, faces crowd pixelated screens, somber and stark in monochrome LED. Caius's voice, clipped and cool, opens the exchange. Eyes track shifting avatars; even the air feels loaded, tense. The city, the hospital, the empire—every kingdom they'd built balanced on the edge of a knife.

"Lucien, what's the verdict?" Caius demands.

"It's worse than we thought," Lucien says, voice brittle but controlled. "They're inside. Double agents, all over the support networks—names embedded in the message I cracked. It's not just surveillance. They're rerouting information, sabotaging us from within."

Darius's face is a mask of quiet fury. "We have hospital personnel accessing data after hours. My own people—colluding. I see it on the tapes. I vouched for these men."

Silas cuts in, every syllable clipped. "Financial assets aren't secure. The theft is surgical. Whoever's behind this is laundering money through our own shell companies, using passwords only my team should possess."

A weighted silence gathers.

Elara breaks it: "So we trust only ourselves now?"

It is Mariel, her voice like broken glass softened by velvet, who issues the warning—her words a reckoning.

"No. We trust *only* those in this circle. Anyone else—no matter their history—is a potential threat. If the rival society has reached this deep, we're at war at home."

On another screen, Lila's hands tremble as she closes her laptop. The world she thought was impenetrable now feels like glass under a hammer, every smile and word from an ally suddenly suspect.

Silence settles, thick as storm clouds, as the realization cuts through each of them—sanctuary is an illusion, and the enemy is already inside.

Deep in the safe house, fluorescence leaks through a crack under the lounge door, spilling pale green light across midnight marble. Shadows breathe inside—the only witnesses as Seraphina steps in, soft footfalls masked by thick carpet. Her eyes have the gleam of steel tempered in fire. Caius sits slouched on the edge of the leather settee, phone in one hand, tension coiled in the other like a wound spring, the half-light knifing a line across his scar. His reflection flickers in the black glass of the window, a sovereign staring at a city he cannot control.

Seraphina crosses her arms, posture unyielding, and traps him there—cornered not by threat, but by a question that stings in her chest. "There's more, isn't there? You held back—about the double agents. About the encrypted network. Why?" Her voice carries the salted edge of sleeplessness, scraping quietly at the silence between them.

Caius doesn't meet her eyes, thumb tapping a restless pattern on the cool leather. The distant hum of optical security—nearly silent, but constant—reminds them both how many ears, digital or not, might be listening. When he finally speaks, his words slide out measured and low. "Some things are safer unknown, Seraphina. I did it for you—for everyone. There's no advantage in sharing every threat if it puts you at greater risk."

Her mouth twists, more wounded than angry. Too many close calls, too many nights walled off from him, heat her words. "You really think you're the only one built for danger? Secrets don't shield us, Caius. They crack us open when the world hits hardest."

He raises his gaze—dark, storm-lit. "I won't have you hunted any more than you already are."

She laughs, sharp and silent. "Too late for that. I'd rather fight with the truth in my hand than stumble blind because you thought I was too precious to trust."

Their standoff tightens, unspoken fears threading the air: What if sharing everything only draws more blood? What if not sharing is what finally breaks them?

On the rooftop, under a roofless black sky, Mariel stands in the thin wind, gaze fixed on distant towers pricked with stars. Lucien's approach is silent, but she senses the taut presence behind her. For a moment, neither speaks, letting nighttime city noise fill the gaps: horns, distant engines, thunder muttering over the skyline.

She turns to him, jaw set. "You think I don't notice? Every time old contacts go silent, every time you change the subject, every time you promise you're 'handling it.' Lucien, what's stalking us isn't gone. It's following us because you won't let the past go."

He pulls in a slow breath, arms folded against the cold. "It's not about letting go. I'm doing what I must to keep you safe. The less you know, the less they can use against you."

Mariel's eyes narrow—accusation sharp, a splinter that finds the nerve. "That's not protection; it's exile. If there's still a ghost moving in our shadows, I need to know. Or is this just you running from it, hoping it never catches up?"

His frustration simmers, voice flaring. "It's not about hope. It's strategy, Mariel." But the words feel empty in his mouth.

Down one corridor, Elara and Orion cut heated shapes in low amber light. Elara, chin lifted, stands between Orion and the stairwell, barring his way. His eyes are molten metal, anger a smolder in every word.

"You shouldn't have been there, Elara. One wrong move, and we both end up dead. I can't—" His voice cracks around the word.

She holds her ground, spine straight. "And what if I hadn't come? You'd have charged in, half-prepared, trusting the first bad lead. I'm not made of glass, Orion. I make my choices—same as you."

He shakes his head, brittle. "There's a difference between brave and reckless. You're becoming too much like me."

"Maybe that's what it takes," she mutters, stepping past him into the shadow.

In the kitchen, under harsh fluorescent light, Hana stands by the table, fingers tightening on a mug of cooling tea. Her voice, normally soft, now steely. "Why do you keep things from me, Silas? Am I just here to smile, or am I truly your partner? You promised honesty."

Silas, pale under the glare, stares at the empty sink. His hands grip the counter, knuckles white. "I wanted to protect you. If you knew what I know—the names, the betrayals—you'd never sleep again. I couldn't bear it."

The kettle clicks off. Hana's shoulders drop. "Maybe that's not your choice to make."

Tension ripples outside the kitchen. Doors shut too loudly. Someone drops a glass—shatter, then stillness.

Later, all gather at the battered dining table, a half-moon of blue screens lighting tired faces. No one meets another's gaze. The air smells faintly of burnt toast, sweat, and coffee gone cold. Each couple drifts inward, voices silenced by what remains unspoken. Suspicion and ache settle like powdered glass, fine and invisible, turning trust fragile as breath. The only sound: the quiet tap-tap of encrypted keys, as the world outside spins on, merciless and unknowing.

Lovers' Interludes

Candlelight flickers along the walls of Seraphina's penthouse, spilling molten gold across the king-size bed. She sits beside Caius at the edge, her fingers tracing the faded scar that cuts a pale path along his cheekbone. The soft hiss and crackle of the city beyond are dulled by sheets of glass, as though the world outside has been banished for these fragile hours.

Caius's hands, strong and broad, rest atop his knees, their edges marred by old injuries. They tremble—barely, but enough that Seraphina notices as she strokes his cheek. The subtle quiver betrays what his voice has not spoken. His shoulders curve inward, defensive against ghosts she can almost see, his breath catching at the edge of each exhale. When he speaks, his words are gravelly, braced by a thousand burdens.

"If I fail them," he murmurs, his voice low and ragged, "I fail you. I built this shield...and now it cracks, and I—" His hands curl on themselves, his jaw tense, eyes burning with frustration and something dangerously close to fear.

Seraphina takes both his hands in hers, pressing her palms firmly to his shaking fingers. Then she leans close, her forehead touching his temple, the scent of her hair clean and warm, candle wax and jasmine. "You're not just a shield, Caius. None of this means anything if you let the armor bury the man inside." Her thumbs sweep light arcs over his knuckles, grounding him as surely as the stars outside anchor the bleeding dusk.

In a breathless hush, she presses a kiss to the edge of his scar. "I see you," she whispers, deliberate and slow. "I always will. Even when you can't." Together they sit, the world narrowed to pulse and skin: his heartbeat, hesitant but undeniable, returning to a steadier rhythm as Seraphina's presence tethers him back from the brink.

Down six stories and half a city away, Mariel leads Lucien through a glass door etched with the faint glimmer of moonlight. The garden behind her research facility is silent but alive—the soil still warm from the day, jasmine grown riotous after spring rain, spreading waxy petals in the dark. Lucien exhales and loosens his tie, his mouth twisting in habitual reserve. The air here is heavier than in his boardrooms, perfumed with blooming things impervious to threat.

Mariel sits, letting the dew-laced bench dampen her skirt. When Lucien hesitates, she pulls him down gently, their shoulders aligning, hands finding one another's. Her fingers, cool where laboratory work has stripped them of callus, thread with his. "Whatever comes for us," she says, her voice barely louder than the rustle of petals, "they can't touch what we've made. I won't let them."

"I want to believe that—" he starts, that unsmiling mask slipping uncertainly.

"Then believe me." Mariel lifts his hand, guiding it to her forearm, where the constellation tattoo glints silver in the moon's pale light.

Lucien studies it, brushing his lips across each inked star, as if offering benediction in silence, the gesture more promise than any vow.

In the hush, Lucien closes his eyes and lets the worry slide from his brow, the scent of jasmine and the press of Mariel's hand knitting a safe space atop the shifting soil.

Far across town, fluorescent halos buzz and flicker outside the office where Lila finds Darius, hunched behind a sheaf of reports, his eyes bloodshot, coat rumpled as if he'd never left the desk. The hospital has a hush broken only by distant monitors and the faint bark of a therapy dog navigating the night shift. Lila, without a word, steps behind Darius's chair—her hands moving to his back, firm and reassuring. He stiffens for a moment, ever the strategist, then sags as her fingers move in gentle circuits, unraveling the coils of stress that have knotted into his spine.

He stands, and she draws him in, his face tucked against her collarbone. Darius shudders—one breath, two, then the tension drains from him, replaced by the fragile trembling of relief. "You shouldn't have to carry this," he says quietly, broken by fatigue. But Lila only holds tighter, a balm against the fevered struggle, her steady heartbeat promising he's not alone.

High above the city's trembling lights, Elara unlocks the cabin's heavy door. Orion stumbles in behind her, rain clinging to the cuffs of his sleeves, his eyes haunted and wild as the wind that batters the eaves. The fire she'd kindled before their arrival throws shifting shadows across the stone hearth, warming the wide-planked floor with a gentle glow.

Orion presses his forehead to hers, seeking grounding as his hands flex at her waist. "What if we're running out of moves?" he murmurs, his voice brittle. Elara only shakes her head, a smile ghosting her lips, and pulls him toward the sofa.

"Then we make new ones." She curls against him, the wool of the throw grazing cold skin, and her hands sketch outlines on his chest as they begin, low-voiced and intertwined, to spin strategies between kisses. Safe here in the mountain hush, the world's siege is a distant thunder, held at bay by warmth and the fragile hope that their plans might hold.

Each couple lingers, hearts synchronized and walls stripped away, sanctuary reclaimed in a world bent on unraveling them. For tonight, love—forged beneath scars and worry—proves the only haven against the shadows closing in.

Hana sits cross-legged on the thick, cream rug, the city's constellation of neon and headlamps smeared against glass like streaks from a distant galaxy. The suite is hushed, each shadow stretching toward the far corners as if reluctant to stray too close. Her toes curl into the silk pile. The scent of rain—sharp, metallic—seeps through an open window, mingling with the faint citrus of her tea cooling beside her.

Silas lingers at the threshold, the cuff of his shirt brushing over the tattooed coil at his wrist. He takes in the room, its quiet radiance trembling at the edge of a world outside that is nothing but alarms and accusations, glass fractured by unseen hands. He exhales—slow, deliberate—but his chest won't loosen; something has him in its jaws tonight.

He crosses to Hana and lowers himself beside her, his knees folding with less grace than she usually sees in him. He lifts his gaze to the city, where towers bleed light over darkened streets and sirens rise, desperate, from far below.

"I can't get the sound of breaking glass out of my head," Silas says. His fingers catch in his hair. "Every time I shut my eyes…I wonder what I missed, what corner I left unguarded. It's as if the walls are shrinking, Hana." The words fracture, softer than he intends. "I don't know how much longer I can keep all of this from caving in."

Hana shifts closer, her knees bumping his. She catches his trembling hand—cool and dry—and cups his cheek, her thumb tracing the line of his jaw as if she can physically anchor him. "You don't have to carry everything alone. Whatever comes…whatever breaks…you and I, we decide what stays intact. They can't touch this—what we are." Her voice, a low song against thunder rattling the windowpane, weaves through the hush.

"I keep replaying all the moments I chose silence over honesty. The nights I told myself I could fix things alone." His chin dips, his eyes closing. "The enemy wants us isolated—wants me isolated—so everything falls from within."

She leans in, her forehead against his. "Then we hold the center," Hana says. "We make this the one place the storm can't reach."

His shoulders loosen. For a heartbeat, they are a universe built for two, suspended between ruin and safety. Outside, the world tears itself apart—executives driven from towers, loyalties bartered for survival, the very heart of the Brotherhood under siege by unknown hands. Silas hears it all: the pulse of unrest that lives in the walls, the hum of betrayal threading the air. Shadows slip at the edge of every moment.

But in here, Hana's fingers on his skin are sanctuary—a promise that not everything has to be defended or hidden to endure.

The city, beyond their windows, is a fever dream: blue lights blinking through rain, the drone of distant helicopters circling evidence of sudden fires. The Brotherhood's name flickers on news feeds, always one step from exposure. Tension seethes on every corner, the old rules—of power, of secrecy, of trust—collapsing in real time.

In these sanctuaries, the world's violence cannot reach. Silas's luxury suite feels like one last stronghold, perched above the abyss. Only within Hana's embrace does he realize the fortress was never concrete or steel, but the quiet persistence of her holding him together when he comes apart.

On a balcony heavy with the scent of coming rain, Seraphina entwines her fingers with Caius's, cool firmness against his calloused palm. She draws him beneath the sweep of starlight and the city's bruised glow. Her thumb sketches circles on the back of his hand. "Let's make a pact," she whispers. "If the world wants to take everything, it will have to come through both of us." Thunder answers, a low growl in the dusk.

Caius looks at her, his eyes dark as the clouds. "Together. Nothing less. Even if it costs everything."

Their words burn into the night—two shadows swearing fealty as the wind sharpens, promising not victory, but a battle fought side by side.

Lila's apartment is scented with cloves, orange peel, and simmering soup. Candlelight flickers against cracked ceramic and soft linen. She hears Darius's key in the lock—footsteps, the subtle exhaustion in their weight. Darius enters, rain dusting his shoulders. His face is drawn, but it softens as Lila hands him a bowl, her smile a small, stubborn star. He breathes in the steam, something like relief blooming in his chest.

"Smells like home," he murmurs, settling across from her.

"Isn't that the point?" she teases, spooning broth. In their laughter, they steal back a fragment of normalcy, a fragile peace ringed by candles, as if light alone could keep the world at bay.

Across the city, Mariel sits curled in a velvet chair, a journal balanced on her knee, Lucien's steady breathing a comfort in the hush. She writes of gratitude, of hope still bright when all else dims. In the golden pool of lamplight, she glances at Lucien's sleeping face, the lines eased from his brow. What they have—what they still might lose—burns sharper than fear. She commits it to paper, weaving defiance with every line.

Night deepens, city and hills dissolving into quiet and shadow. Within each refuge, hands remain intertwined, breaths shared. Love—here, now—is shield and anchor, the final sanctuary against the siege gathering beyond the glass.

Night presses in heavily against the mountain cabin's windows, clouds sinking low and thick over the slopes. Inside, firelight pulses against raw stone while Elara, silhouetted by a trembling lattice of moon and flame, sits on the wide windowsill. Wind bends the pines, and sometimes distant thunder rumbles, a small echo of the storms inside her.

Her hands twist in her lap. She stares out, her jaw tight, eyelids fluttering against tears she will not let fall—her gaze tracking something unnamed beyond the glass, something that could reach in and tear Orion away without warning. Across the quiet room, Orion watches her. He stands as if undecided, rooted by the hearth, fingers laced absently over his tattooed forearm, pulse leaping beneath ink.

"Elara." His voice catches, rough as gravel scoured by rain. "Talk to me. Don't keep me out."

She doesn't move for a breath, then: "You say you'll always come back. But what if one day you can't?" The words spill out before she can shape them into something softer, and her throat tightens. "Every time you leap—every fight, every scheme, every reckless promise—I cannot breathe until I see you standing again." She meets his gaze; in her eyes, the fire flickers fierce and scared.

Orion crosses the room in two strides. He kneels, his hands on her knees, his own trembling. "I'm here. I'll always find my way to you. I can't promise sense or safety—not every time—but I swear I'll fight to stay."

"I'm not asking for promises you can't keep." Her fingers slip into his hair, curling at the nape of his neck. "But I can't be brave for both of us, not if you won't let yourself be afraid too." Her voice fractures, small. "Let me carry some of it. Or I'll drown."

He presses his forehead to hers, his breath warm and trembling. "Then take it. I'd be lost without you anyway."

She lets her silence say what words can't—her arms slide around him, holding him fiercely as if grounding herself to the earth and anchoring him against the violence of his own heart.

In the city far below, Lucien's penthouse office glows dimly with blue-white light. Lucien sits at his desk, his hands folded as if on trial before a silent jury. Mariel leans against the edge, her presence steady, the scent of jasmine—somehow clinging to her from their earlier walk—threading the sterile air.

He lifts his eyes, haunted hollows. "Years ago, I believed loyalty was stronger than fear. I was wrong. I trusted a man—my right hand. He sold us out for the price of a quiet night. Everything I built nearly burned to ruin. I nearly lost myself." His thumb rubs the gold band on his hand, thinking of everything lost and gained.

Mariel's hand envelops his in gentle steadiness. "You're not that man now. Your wounds—your secrets—don't make you weak." She squeezes, soft but certain. "Let it weigh less. You don't have to hold it alone."

He feels the old tension unclench, a guarded breath finally released. "I want to trust. I want to be the man you see."

"You already are."

Across the city, Seraphina paces, her bare feet silent on the plush carpet that soaks up the blue-gold city glow spilling through her penthouse windows. Her hair tumbles loose, wild around her face, her jaw set.

She whirls, her hands clenched. "I want to believe in the path you've chosen, Caius—I love you, I do. But what if it's the wrong one? What if protecting your brothers this way means losing everything else?"

Caius stands silent, his posture stiff, vulnerability flaring in his olive-dark eyes. For once, his calm cracks. "Tell me I'm not blind. Tell me I'm not leading us into ruin."

She stops in front of him then, her chest rising and falling fast, and lets her guard drop. "Just let me see, Caius. Let me share the weight or I'll be crushed by it, too."

After a moment, his arms enfold her, his voice lower. "We'll walk this together. I'll show you every step I still have strength to take—and every fear."

She melts into his embrace—just for tonight, honesty razoring away everything but the thudding of their hearts.

A storm laces the windows of Silas's suite, lightning flashing violet on high-gloss floors. Silas stands rigid, his knuckles white on the frame, recalling that last night—the one where his secrets nearly got Hana killed. He cannot look at her, shame curving his spine.

"I failed you," he murmurs, his voice thin as glass. "I kept the truth hidden, and you paid the price."

Hana steps forward, her eyes shining. She cups his cheek, her thumb sweeping the jagged scar. "Your mistakes aren't the sum of you. We are not finished because of what's past." Tears shimmer but do not fall. "You are more than your fear."

His defenses buckle; her forgiveness seeps into him, gentle as rain smoothing old stone. He rests his forehead against hers, allowing himself this fragile absolution.

In each quiet sanctuary, doubt and dread coil and retreat, replaced by a raw, wordless understanding. The air vibrates with unsaid vows. Tonight, in the hush between storms, honesty and broken courage create something unbreakable—a promise lived in linked hands and the slow, measured breathing of lovers who know the darkness outside is waiting, but who, for now, have only each other to hold.

Caius Accused

The private meeting room thrums with anticipation, every reflective granite surface gleaming under the careful haze of recessed amber lights. The city beyond the thick walls is a blur of neon, but here, time compresses into the metallic ring of silence. The Brotherhood sits hushed around the blackened oak conference table, constellation emblems winking on leather chairs. The only movement is the faint flicker of jackets and the subtle tightening of hands, knuckles pale against mahogany. A single crystal decanter stands untouched, refracting prismatic slivers onto stacks of crisp, unmarked paper.

The courier appears as a mere shadow slipping through the threshold—a thin man, anonymous beneath a cap, carrying a plain sealed envelope. No flourish, no words, only the persistent stamp of expensive shoes on marble. He vanishes the moment the package is claimed, the security doors hissing closed behind him like a serpent's sigh.

Orion, jaw tight, breaks the seal. Darius accepts the documents, eyes narrowed as he shuffles through dense columns of transaction codes and timestamps. Lucien lifts the USB, its slick surface cold against his fingertips, and connects it to the conference tablet. The screen flickers, then steadies. Caius doesn't speak. The heat of a hundred old betrayals presses against his skin, but he holds himself motionless—a hinge between worlds.

Static fizzes. Then, a voice: deep, measured. It wears Caius's inflections like a tailored suit, negotiating through each damning line. The words drip with the cadence of long, private conversations—terms, numbers, names. On the screens, transfer slips lace together empires with the sterile brutality of accounting. The table grows colder. No one reaches for the glass; no one glances up. Even Silas's face, usually unreadable, is drawn and pale beneath the steeled veneer.

A line of tension thrums through the room. Every ear sharpens, every breath shallow, punctuated by the low hum of the air system and the static pop between sentences on the recording. The voice implicates Caius in bribery, in secrets traded for cash, in the architecture of betrayal. The Brotherhood has survived assassins, blackmail, and hostile takeovers—but this? The enemy has found a way in.

Footsteps echo beyond, quick and purposeful—Seraphina, summoned and golden in the artificial light. She pauses in the threshold, assessing the rigid storm of the room, her gaze snagging on Caius's stoic profile. Her presence cracks the silence, the scent of wild jasmine drifting with her.

"Caius?" Her voice is edged, fierce.

He stands. The words—impossible to swallow—taste of old iron. "You need to hear something." He gestures to the screen and sets the USB in motion again, each syllable stabbing at the delicate membrane of intimacy between them.

She listens, her face shifting from shock to furious disbelief. She points to the papers on the table, her hands trembling—but her voice never falters. "If you want me to stand here and accept this, I want every second of evidence, every file, every origin signature. Who sent this? Who touched it? There's not a soul here who doesn't know how easily things can be doctored."

Darius leans forward, eyes dark. "Seraphina, there are signatures—all matching Caius's own encryption."

She bristles, chin high. "Computers can do what men cannot. I want to see the files."

Orion's voice cracks—harsh, defensive. "This reeks of tampering. Who would believe Caius would risk all this for—" He stops short, his eyes scanning each face for a hint of collusion.

"Not everything is as it seems, Orion," Silas interrupts, slow and measured. "But until we know more, no one is above suspicion. Not even him."

A silence settles, taut as piano wire. The only sound is Lucien's steady, controlled breathing.

Caius, hands unmoving at his sides, feels every gaze pierce through him. Suspicion, confusion, disappointment—a constellation of grief. He's memorized these men's strengths, their flaws, their loyalty—studied the iron rules that once made them invincible. The Brotherhood has always been a fortress built upon relentless discipline: biometric locks, surveillance so sophisticated it shamed foreign intelligences, an internal code stricter than blood. Every threat has been cataloged, every past betrayal shut out.

But now he sees it—all that rigor can't keep this poison out. The windows here are bulletproof, the walls thick, but trust is thinner than glass.

I didn't do this. I would never. The argument plays silent, desperate, in Caius's mind, his pulse echoing the metallic taste in his mouth. Who is clever enough to fool their failsafes? What message is this, delivered in the language of their own undoing? Beneath his composure, panic steals through his veins—his empire teeters, but so does his life with Seraphina. If they fracture, nothing survives.

He looks up, locking on Seraphina's face. In her eyes: a hurricane, a hundred unspoken I believe you's braced against a world that won't. He's never needed her faith more than now; his power, once absolute, slips through his grasp, icy and irreversible.

One by one, the Brotherhood rises. The swish of suit fabric, the snap of folders—each man clutching evidence as if it might bite. Eyes evade Caius, save for Seraphina, whose grip on the damning documents shakes. Tension crackles, heavier than stone.

The meeting scatters, the hush lingering behind. Seraphina stays, lips pressed white against secrets she refuses to surrender, her hands trembling as the doors sigh shut.

Marble gleams beneath Seraphina's bare feet as she strides down labyrinthine corridors, the night air cool on her skin, the headquarters whispering with restless secrets. Her hand tightens on the encrypted laptop, knuckles paling, as the door slides shut behind her and locks her into the hush of her quarters. The city's lights pulse through distant glass; tension rides the electric hush, each sound edged with threat. The room smells faintly of jasmine from a crushed blossom on her desk—its sweetness almost suffocating.

Mariel is the first to arrive, footsteps measured against the stone, her dark eyes sharp and threaded with worry. Lila follows, hair mussed from haste, a soft shadow against the teal-lit walls. The three women form a deliberate triangle around the low table as Seraphina powers the laptop and plugs in the evidence. Blue-white light flickers over digital records; static breathes from the speakers as the evidence loads, a sound that prickles at every nerve.

Seraphina's hands fly over the keys. She can feel the weight of expectation pressing into her shoulders with every keystroke. Failure is a poison in the air, unspoken but thick. Doubt dogs her, but she clamps it down; every movement is an act of defiance against fear.

"Start here—voice samples. Compare the cadence. The modulation. Anything that feels... wrong," she murmurs, her voice hoarse from sleeplessness.

"Let me run a filter for generated artifacts," Mariel says. Her fingers span with elegant precision across the trackpad, windows multiplying, graphs pulsing. Her eyes narrow. "This section—listen. That break—almost imperceptible." The speaker emits a clipped distortion—one a human ear might miss, but Mariel does not. "AIs stutter precisely there. It's subtle, but code leaves fingerprints."

Lila angles her head, scrolling through printouts. "These transfer codes—Caius never uses this format. Bank logs, two are out of pattern, and this signature hash is off." Her finger taps the screen, nail clicking. "Someone built this to fool us, but they slipped."

Heat pools at the base of Seraphina's spine—a living thing, hope and adrenaline. She tries to speak, but the words tangle.

"Could the others believe this so easily?" Lila's murmur is half anger, half heartache.

Mariel's tone is measured, a counterweight to Seraphina's storm. "They want something—a reason to doubt. Or maybe they're just scared."

"I have to bring this to them." Seraphina's voice hardly sounds like her own.

The sun has not yet burned away the city's haze when they gather in the senior council's office. Frosted glass hides the outside world, but the air vibrates with arguments unsaid. Orion leans forward, fists braced on his knees; Lucien sits rigid, eyes flinty. A cold, lemon tang of sanitizer rides the sterile air, but underneath, the musky note of old leather and the faint bitter reek of tension linger.

Seraphina loads her findings onto the wall monitor. The room's attention swings to the screen.

"Listen—here and here." Mariel's voice drapes through the air, layered with authority. "It's not him."

"We have trace AI modulation in the audio," Seraphina says, blood thrumming. "Financial signatures—faked. This is planted. Please. All I'm asking is time. Don't let them turn us against each other."

Orion releases a snort through his nose, jaw working. "It reeks of setup. Anyone not see it?"

Lucien's reply is colder, more surgical. "We can't afford to ignore a breach. Not now. Every protocol needs auditing. Every file, every access point. No exceptions."

"It's Caius. That doesn't make sense. Why would he—" Orion's voice cracks, angrier at doubt than at anyone present.

Silas, shadowed and distant, shakes his head. "This isn't just outside interference. Someone inside knows how we move. We wouldn't have let it get this far otherwise."

"So what, we hang him before we know?" Orion's words cut through the hush.

Lucien answers, low, "We suspend judgment. Not loyalty, not yet. But we act. Otherwise, we're already dead."

Silas's eyes are cold sea glass. "Too many second chances. Remember where that led us, Lucien?"

The room thickens, silence dense with everything unsaid.

Seraphina wants to scream, to shake them until old trust wakes. She doesn't. Her hands tremble on the table's edge.

Suspicion fractures the meeting as members peel away, voices too soft and heads bowed. Groups splinter, the old guard glancing sidelong at the newer faces, everyone clutching their own version of certainty. The air reeks of exhaustion and doubt, of expensive cologne gone sour. Seraphina stands alone at the table, watching pixelated evidence blink on the monitor—her knuckles white, hope and fear gnawing their way up her throat.

She imagines the schism—the Brotherhood shattered into rival camps, every loyalty suspect, Caius exiled or worse. What if she fails? What's left if truth can't rise above clever lies? Her reflection in the blank monitor—tired, unbowed—dares her not to flinch.

Yet seedlike, a sliver of hope pulses: that justice, found and fiercely defended, could be an act that changes more than just tonight. Maybe, if she holds fast, trust can be rebuilt from these fault lines. Maybe love, not fear, forges the new constellation ahead.

But none of this matters if, by dawn, she can't deliver the proof that saves them all.

In the back corner of the downtown club, the air sits heavy with the scent of tobacco and aged whisky, a haze stitched together by low murmurs and the clink of crystal tumblers. Shadows lap at the velvet, hiding more than faces; they veil secrets. Darius sits across from Silas at a table disguised by darkness, his posture relaxed but alert, dark eyes never quite leaving the man opposite. Silas, lean and angular, keeps his fingers tracing the rim of his untouched glass, his blue gaze darting from Darius to the jagged mirror behind the bar, as if expecting truth to crawl out of the reflection.

A jazz number coils through the hush, muted brass and midnight piano. Their words, when they come, swim just above a whisper.

"They want blood for this," Darius says, keeping his voice level, eyes flickering as candlelight catches the scar on Silas's jaw. "You know I trust Caius."

Silas speaks softly, but each syllable is weighed, deliberate. "Trust isn't blind. Not after what happened three years ago. You remember how quickly faith can be bartered for survival."

Darius shifts, the polished table cool beneath his calloused hands. "That's exactly why we have to hold the line now. If we fracture—"

"The Brotherhood was fractured long before this." Silas's mouth tightens, drawing near to bitterness. "Caius drew the line. But you saw how they looked at him, even as evidence burned in their hands."

"If we let poison take root, there'll be nothing left to save." Darius's voice deepens, patience threaded with warning.

A silence stretches, thick as fog. Glasses sweat on lacquer. Shadows ripple and settle again.

Silas finally meets Darius's gaze, his fingers pausing. "Suppose you're wrong? Suppose he's not the man you think?"

"I'd stake everything on him," Darius says, not flinching. "Would you?"

Silas's answer hangs unspoken as the music swells, then fades.

Only years of shared history, of alliances forged beneath fire and threat, keep this conversation from unraveling. There's a story in every careful glance: Darius, steady as stone, refusing to let suspicion chip away at memory, and Silas, haunted, hearing echoes of betrayal in every concession. Darius remembers nights when trust went up in smoke—hospital staff sabotaged, files vanished, a silent enemy wearing a trusted face. The ordeal shaped him, forced him to see how treachery flowers in shadow. Now, watching Silas, he recognizes something brittle under the man's iron composure: fear, not of outside enemies, but of wounds reopening within.

It's the same lesson Darius can't shake—no fortress is impregnable when loyalty itself is hollowed by doubt. His partnership with Lila taught him the cost of vigilance, the loneliness of constant watchfulness. He's learned to mask his caution with gentleness, to trust where he can, even as past betrayals whisper that every friend could be turned by the right leverage or threat.

Later, under the blinking sodium lights in the city's underbelly, Orion strides into the Brotherhood's safehouse, footsteps echoing above the hum of hidden servers and recycled air. Lucien sits at a console, posture rigid, the blue screen glow reflecting from his watchful eyes. Orion's frustration is a palpable thing—a coiled storm.

"They're pinning it on Caius now? You actually believe this crap?" Orion's tone bristles, jaw taut.

Lucien's fingers drum once on the table. "I trust the man. Not the evidence. And not the timing. This—" he gestures sharply, "—is a game designed to play us against ourselves."

"Then we need to fight it. Shut down the leaks, cut off the rumors." Orion rakes a hand through his hair. "Whoever did this knows us. Knows how to split us up."

Lucien doesn't rise to the heat, but his words carry warning. "Old ghosts have been rattling the windows for years. It doesn't take much to let them in. You want to fix this? Watch your back, and make sure you're not the one being used."

"They can try," Orion growls, low and dangerous. "But I know where my loyalty lives."

Lucien's eyes narrow, measuring, but he nods once—a brief flicker of alliance. "Meet me at first light. We run an internal check. No one outside. Understood?"

A world away, Lila weaves through hospital corridors scented with antiseptics and cut blooms, her footsteps padded on green tile. She rounds a corner and catches wind of two junior associates, their backs hunched, words sharp and hushed.

"He sounded guilty," one says, fear biting at the edges. "If Caius goes down, we're finished."

Lila pauses, breath held—not for the content, but for the venom riding it. She glides past, pulling out her phone. Her message to Seraphina is hidden behind an innocuous emoji—one practiced code between sisters-in-arms. Rumors spread like infection. She won't let them fester unseen.

Elsewhere, in a dim office shuttered to sunlight, an elder councilman's growl scratches at old scars. "We forgave once," he rasps, eyes glinting above the rim of his tumbler. "And paid the price. Consider where your loyalties truly lie before you choose what ruins us next."

Dusk settles outside. Fingers slip a note from palm to palm among men clustered by the iron fence in the park. A single word scorched in ink beneath Caius's name: traitor.

The office adjoining the Brotherhood's war room breathes with a tight, electric stillness. Towers of dossiers and half-finished reports litter a midnight-gleaming desk—paper edges curled like claws. Low light glances off the black marble floors, turning every movement ghostly and insubstantial. Already, the air tastes of adrenaline and copper, something cold and metallic where memories of laughter and victory should dwell.

Seraphina steps inside, pulse racing, finding Caius turned away from her, hands white-knuckled around the edge of the desk. The tension in his back telegraphs more than words. On the other side of the thick glass, the city glimmers—but in here, their world contracts to the muted silence of fear and accusation.

She closes the door a touch too hard—just enough for him to flinch, shoulders tightening as if bracing for a blow. Even now, the ghost of him—her anchor, her storm—feels distant. She stares at his broad silhouette, searching somewhere beneath the surface for proof solid as stone, something only she can sense.

"I want to believe you," she starts, her voice brittle, each word a shard she struggles to release. "I do. But they keep looking at you—at us—like the verdict's written. It buries me, Caius. I can't shake these doubts. Even when I swear I'll die before I let them win."

He finally turns, his face drawn sharper in the lamplight. The old scar on his cheek glows paler against his olive skin, and when he meets her eyes, she sees the abyss—fear raw as an open wound, hope threading its way through ruin.

"You think I haven't asked myself," he says quietly, his voice carrying splinters. "If I missed something. If one of my own—someone I trusted—set this in motion. Seraphina, I built all of this so we'd never face a night like this. I thought I'd outplanned them all." He rakes a hand through his hair, his gaze landing somewhere beyond her on the empty wall. "But now—if I lose you, or the Brotherhood—if we fracture because of this, what have I ever been, except a fool gambling with people's lives?"

She steps in, close enough to sense the tremor that runs through him, close enough to recognize his pulse echoing the same frantic rhythm as her own. A scent of vetiver clings to his suit, and beneath it, the stress musk of fear and sleeplessness.

"They've turned us on each other," she murmurs, almost to herself. "That's the real weapon, isn't it? Not the files, not the voices—just suspicion, worming through us all." She lifts her chin, challenging the ghosts haunting him. "I don't care how real that evidence looks. I know you. I know what you'll fight for."

"And if the others don't?" His hand lifts helplessly before falling open at his side.

"They can't decide what I believe," she whispers. "Not about you. We'll prove them wrong. Or burn trying."

The corridor blurs with rushed steps, brief murmurs—summoning them. Caius's eyes stay on Seraphina as they move together, both bracing, both brittle. The marrow of the night carries them onward, fear rising thick as incense.

In the circular war room, amber sconces paint skin and marble in solemn gold. The high-backed chairs ring the black oak table like silent sentinels. Projected high on the domed ceiling, the Brotherhood's constellation sparkles faintly, cold and remote. The others gather: Lucien's face masked in calculation, Darius's jaw set, Orion radiating restless energy. Silas sits in reserved darkness, his eyes flicking to shadows.

A council member speaks, voice low and heavy, each word dragging. "We have to suspend Caius. We can't let doubt rot us from the inside. There will be an internal review."

Silence blooms, thick and uneasy as curdled cream.

Orion smashes a fist to the table. "You're accusing him on doctored tapes and spreadsheets. We know how easily those can be twisted."

Lucien's response is quiet, the edge of steel unmistakable. "It's not just the evidence. It's that we've let our guard slip, let old wounds fester." He glances at Caius, regret flickering behind the mask. "If we don't act now, they'll bury us."

Darius clears his throat. "We need clarity, not chaos. But until we find the hand behind this, we should give Caius the benefit of the doubt—not declare him a traitor."

Silas leans forward, his voice softened by fatigue, not surrender. "Every empire falls to betrayal that starts at home. If we ignore this, we could be signing our own death warrants."

The surge of argument ricochets—a volley of wounded pride and fear. The words barely mask the mistrust growing like mold beneath their unity. One by one, alliances fracture along fine, invisible lines. Only Seraphina stands at Caius's side, her solidity a beacon in the crumbling darkness.

No voice rises to consensus. The meeting dissolves with each tense breath, the Brotherhood's emblem—once a symbol of brotherhood and promise—casting cold, flickering constellations across faces turned away from one another. No one moves to extinguish the light.

And as the last echoes fade, the future dangles on the edge of a blade, poised to fall or splinter beyond mending.

Midnight Blackmail

Lucien locks his study door as midnight's hush settles over the penthouse. The windowpane glimmers with city light, fractured gold and neon blue, casting haphazard shadows across the thick rugs and the sharp lines of his mahogany desk. The air is heavy with the clean chill of filtered ozone—Lucien always demands purity and control—yet his hands tremble faintly as he slides into his chair. He draws in a breath. The old wound beneath his left cheek tingles, a phantom memory awakened by tension.

He taps his encrypted terminal awake. The screen flares in the dim room, throwing reflected light against polished wood and glass. There—one message, nested beneath layers of security even Orion would admire. Its subject line is a single star. When he opens it, a pulse of static fills his ears: distorted, malicious. Someone has taken his voice—sliced, tortured, and rebuilt it with digital ice, so each word stabs: "You know what you owe—pay, or Mariel's blood will answer."

The words hang in the room, electric and raw. He can hear his own heartbeat in the silence that follows, the heavy, irregular thump echoing up through his chest into his throat. The city's rumble filters up from sixty stories below—a distant, indifferent pulse. Lucien swallows. Static crackles from the speakers as he opens the second file. He scrolls through the demand, each instruction as precise and cold as a scalpel: Transfer research files from Project Astra to the attached offshore account, sign documentation surrendering full ownership of the research subsidiary, and do it by sunrise. If not—all the dark, unburied things from the underworld past he has spent years walling away will surface. Names, records, violence. Mariel.

A fine sweat beads at his temples. Lucien stares down at his hands, knuckles pale against the gunmetal keys. For a moment, all the composure he wears like armor shatters. His mind swirls with memory—a flash of blood in an alley, the press of steel against his face, the cold bite of betrayal when a partner's eyes turned glassy with fear. Even now, after so many years, scars like that ache in the marrow of him. He remembers how he carved his place through brute strategy and merciless survival, each choice layering guilt and skill like sediment on the ocean floor.

If he obeys the threat, Mariel survives—but the Brotherhood will never trust him again, and everything they have built together will corrode from within. If he resists, the blackmailer's so-called insurance—a grainy recording, an autopsy photo, the hint of a name—could ignite violence and exile. Worst of all, the thin tether of safety he has constructed around Mariel will snap.

He clenches his fists until his palms sting. Tell Mariel? Bring the Brotherhood in? No. He can almost feel Caius's gaze, sharp as a hawk: Are you still a liability or a brother? The shame stings sharper than any threat.

Glass shatters—wet, sudden—sending shards bouncing across the marble. Lucien's arm vibrates. Only then does he realize he has hurled his water tumbler at the far wall. Cold liquid spreads beneath an abstract painting; amber light dapples across the mess. He bows his head, fighting back the panic growing wild inside him.

The door creaks. Slippers on the rug. Mariel enters, wrapped in a fall of midnight hair, her expression alert and shadowed by lamp glow. He senses her before she speaks, her presence an anchor; the faint scent of rosemary from her evening tea lingers in her wake.

"What happened?" Her voice is velvet flint, edged with worry. She spots the glass, the terminal's glow still slicing the dark.

"It's nothing. Just—go back to bed." Lucien's voice sounds brittle, foreign in his own mouth.

"It's never nothing at midnight, Lucien," she says, stepping across the fractured spill. Her tone changes—softer, but unyielding. "Don't you dare shut me out. Not tonight."

He remains rigid, mouth tight. The words choke at the back of his throat—terror, confession, shame; none will pass. Silence presses between them, thick as fog.

"I heard your voice from the hallway. You were talking to someone." She studies his face, her own haunted just as surely by worry as his is by regret. "Show me."

She reaches for his hand. At first, he resists, tension locking every muscle. But her fingers are warm, certain, grounding him. Something in him breaks. He faces her ghosts with his own.

"Mariel—" He manages her name, raw. "They want everything. They want the Brotherhood, the research, our future. And if I don't give it, they'll hurt you. I swore this would never touch you."

She kneels beside his chair, her palm pressing over his. "You don't get to decide that alone anymore."

He gasps, as if surfacing from deep water. For a moment, he's only a man, stripped of calculations.

"I'm not leaving you to face this. Not ever."

Lucien closes his eyes. She is the only star left in his midnight sky.

The afternoon city is thick with moisture and the slow churn of traffic, but back here—behind the jewel-box glass and brushed steel of Lucien and Mariel's residence—the world narrows to the loaded hush of service alleys and the hum of distant security gates. Shadows grow longer, sharpened by the low sun glancing off chrome rails and concrete. It's not the first time Mariel has moved like this, hovering between the comfort of home and the wild territory of risk. The rear exit's security lamp flickers feebly overhead, casting the two men below into jittery, fragmented silhouettes.

They stand by the recycling bins, heads angled low, burner phones pressed to their mouths. One man's suit is too stiff, his stance too rehearsed. She marks it instantly; not delivery crew, not doormen—outsiders with an agenda. Language slips from their lips in clipped, code-laden murmurs.

Seventeen A. Gavel's in motion. The master expects the professor's data by dusk.

Adrenaline climbs through her, sharp as the scent of ozone after a clean storm. She fits herself against the wall, moving in a practiced half-crouch, shoes silent on damp concrete. In the space between the security cameras' sweep, she focuses on her breath the way she learned after that warehouse stakeout last winter, when the Brotherhood's safety depended on keeping calm under fire. Every muscle is hyper-aware. Every trick is drilled through failure and repetition. Trust the angles, the soundscape, the smallest shiver betraying intent.

She's learned to read lips at a glance. To split audio fragments in her mind, isolate danger in the background noise—a lesson hard-won from nights spent in soundproofed cars, earpiece pressed close, Lucien's voice steadying her nerves. Even now, she fights down the memory of blood on frosted glass and Siren alarms, focusing instead on the tiny red light blinking at her thumb: phone recording, live.

She edges between parked trucks, the grit grinding beneath her fingertips as she steadies herself against a metal bumper. Voices crackle, words carved with careful dread.

No deviation. Tonight or not at all. The master wants leverage.

We've got surveillance rotating, but there's another sweep at five. Let's not get caught in the net.

It's clear—the message, the underlying threat. Mariel lets her mind spool through the recent chain of attacks: a glove left on their car, code scratched into her elevator button, the encrypted email Lucien never truly explained. Each pattern fractures and reforms in her thoughts, converging on one certainty—these men answer to something larger, a shadow that circles their lives now with teeth bared.

For a moment, scenery blurs into the tunnel vision of memory: the time she tailed a blackmailer through old Parisian tunnels, nerves unraveling with every echo but remaining anchored by the mechanics of trust. Her training returns—never hug the corners, always check your six, keep one escape route mapped under your tongue. Today the stakes bleed into every inch of her resolve: Lucien's haunted eyes at dawn, the tremor she recognized in his protected calm.

A step crunches behind her. One man half-turns, suspicion riding the angle of his jaw. Mariel freezes, profile tight against a battered trunk. She counts to three, muscles making themselves small, then slides her phone behind her back, angling the microphone outward just enough. The familiar taste of fear—metallic, swift—blooms on her tongue, yet she doesn't falter. She shifts, waits for their attention to return to their argument. When it does, she retreats, slipping out just as a security patrol's heavy boots echo down the corridor.

Inside the service elevator, silence presses hard and bright. Her breath comes quick, condensed in visible streams as the cool recirculated air meets her heated skin. Legs tense, she sends the audio file and a burst of covertly snapped photos to Lucien's encrypted line. Her message is crisp, annotated: two external agents, burner phones, reference to "professor's data," triangulate for connection to last night's directive. She resists the urge to pace as the carriage rises, the metallic hum an odd comfort amid uncertainty.

Her phone vibrates—Lucien's warning flashes across the screen, stern and achingly familiar.

Do not get involved; it's too dangerous.

Her thumb hesitates. Doubt tugs at her, coiling with the urge to obey, to retreat into the safety of Lucien's shadow. But another voice presses back, stubborn and certain: he's not the only one with something to lose. Loyalty isn't silent compliance. It's standing shoulder to shoulder when the wolves come for blood.

She types, hands steady despite the flame in her chest.

With you, not behind you.

A code they wrote together. Their promise.

As she steps from the elevator back into the labyrinth of alleys, the sun has shifted, painting the concrete with long gold stripes. She spots the matte-black vehicles—Brotherhood surveillance, purring quietly in the shade, engine heat rippling above the hoods. Relief loosens her spine. Whatever storm waits in the shadows, she isn't out here alone.

Light presses through the coffeehouse's tinted windows, thick with the aroma of ground beans and scorched caramel. The din of the city recedes behind layers of concrete and reinforced glass, but Lucien feels the pulse of old dangers crawling up his spine. The bell above the entry tings—a sound loaded with childhood memories, midnight meetings, and coded signals. His heart pounds, a cold throb beneath crisp white linen.

He has already clocked the exits, the cameras in their domed shells, the glint of a knife behind the counter. Every movement is muscle memory. At a far-back table, a hunched figure watches crème swirl in his coffee, gaze restless. Nikolai—the man Lucien once called friend and, more precisely, shield. His suit is rumpled, hands shaking so that the spoon clinks and echoes, sharp as a heartbeat. Lucien sits. The chair groans.

Nikolai drags a hand through thinning hair. "You came. Thought maybe you'd just send a cleaner."

"I don't send anyone to bury old ghosts," Lucien murmurs, eyes dark as storm glass. "Not when they've come calling."

Their words tangle in the tick of the antique wall clock. Stale pastries, burnt sugar, the bitterness of too-dark roast seep into the fabric of the room. Lucien waits, chest tight, every cell screaming for this to be over, planned and controlled. But the past refuses the leash.

Nikolai swallows. "They wrote to me. Used the name—your old code, from the docks." His hands ball into fists. "They know about the deal. All of it. The girl, the gun. What you buried."

Lucien stiffens. Images flicker: sodium light washing over broken crates, the slap of wet cement, blood streaming from a rent in someone's scalp, pooling at his feet as he choked orders into his comm. He had thought it contained—a bad memory, locked away behind layers of silence and payoffs, a thing best forgotten and sealed by dirt and fear.

But history claws its way out. Years ago, there was a shipment—synthetics, cutting-edge tech, military grade, off the books, off the grid. The Brotherhood's reach was still raw and grasping then, and Lucien's ambition desperate to impress. He was supposed to close the deal, oversee the transfer, but greed and paranoia twisted everything. Rivals ambushed the hand-off. Screams fractured the air. Shots rang out. In the chaos, a civilian went down—a girl in the wrong place, her red scarf slick with blood. Someone had to take the fall. The Brotherhood couldn't show its face. Lucien did what he did best: cleaned house, rewrote the story, paid the right officials, fed the right lies. The trial became theater, all evidence pointing elsewhere. Nikolai kept quiet. Lucien orchestrated the chorus. The secret never saw daylight—until now.

He locks eyes with Nikolai, voice brittle. "You didn't tell them anything?"

"No. God, Lucien, I'm not an idiot. But they offered... things. Threatened the kid. Showed me photos of my wife on her commute." The man shudders. "They want details. They said your name, your role. My silence comes with a timer."

Lucien closes his eyes, feeling shame uncoil in his stomach. That old world—he had left it behind in blood and marble, or so he had convinced himself. But loose threads never stay hidden. Sweat beads at his neck despite the air conditioning, the ghosts of old choices pressing in, breath hot, asking what he owes and to whom.

He murmurs, "I'll handle this. You and your family—leave the city. Take the money. Don't talk. I'll contact you when it's safe."

Nikolai doesn't thank him. He nods, stands, and is gone, leaving Lucien with the taste of acrid fear.

A moment later, Mariel enters the back room. The hush that falls is heavy enough to suffocate. She sits beside Lucien—close, legs angled toward him, her eyes probing as though searching for an answer in shadow.

He looks at her, and the shield he has carried all day shatters. Another secret slips between them. "You wanted the truth," he starts, but his voice cracks, raw. "There was a night, years ago. A deal gone wrong. The kind that stains everything. I lied to save the Brotherhood, covered a murder. Bribed the court. Let an innocent be forgotten. That's what they're holding over me now."

He pauses, grinding his palms into the edge of the table until his skin burns. "If it comes out, everything unravels—my reputation, the Brotherhood, our lives. But it's worse than that. If they name you as my partner, you're a target. I thought I could fence the past behind walls. It never works. I'm sorry—I'm so damn sorry."

For a long, aching minute, Mariel just breathes, her lips white, hands twisting. Finally, she rests her palm over his—soft, certain, unyielding even as her eyes glisten. The words come quietly but cut through the static. "Lucien, you gave me your trust. Your past doesn't define you. I see the man you've become. You don't carry this alone. Not anymore."

Lucien turns, folding her into his arms, every part of him trembling with relief and dread and the stubborn, unkillable hope that somehow, for her, he can shed the old darkness. For now, in the charged hush of the coffeehouse, they hold each other as tightly as the world allows.

They meet in the home office, dusk washing the windows in burnt amber and indigo. Light dips through the city skyline, bleeding fractured shadows across mahogany shelves lined with relics—an ancient chess set, a brass sextant, a dragonfly caught in resin. Lucien stands rigid near the whiteboard, his skin pale against the twilight. On the glass, he has drawn a web of names and encrypted codes, red marker encircling the blackmailer's demands. Mariel, exhausted but unbowed, uncaps a blue pen and adds arrows, connecting aliases and offshore accounts in quick, decisive strokes. The air holds a metallic edge. Distant city sirens bleed into the hush, underscored by the low, pulsing thrum of the apartment's reinforced security systems.

Lucien's hands hover at his sides, uncertain. He watches Mariel's reflection in the window; her posture is tense but purposeful, chin up, hair pulled tight. He wonders when trust stopped feeling like a liability and began to taste like necessity. His whole life he has played the shadow—half-seen, never fully exposed. He never imagined anyone would see him this raw. Yet Mariel's presence steadies him, her measured breath drawing him back from the brink.

Mariel circles back to Lucien, papers rustling in her grip. She doesn't glance at the scar on his cheek or the fatigue arranging itself beneath his eyes. Instead, she points to the outline they have built—a false trail, an electronic honeypot primed to catch anyone who bites.

"If we feed them the dummy files here," Mariel says, voice low but sure, "we can implant a beacon. If they open even one string, our firewall will ping their IP—hopefully before they realize we're onto them."

Lucien nods, but there's a tremor in his jaw. "If they realize too soon, they'll go after you." The taste of copper anxiety climbs the back of his throat. "Or escalate to the Brotherhood."

Mariel's lips press together. She steps closer, offering him the blue pen, her brow knitted.

"You can't shield us both by pulling away," she says. "I want to be part of this—not stashed behind a wall of half-truths." She leans in, searching his face, her hand—cool, unsparing—settling on his wrist. "If you're going to war, you don't go without me."

For a moment, Lucien closes his eyes, fighting the old instinct to deny, to cage every secret behind dignity and steel. A storm of memories surges—Nikolai's haunted accusations, the lawyer's blood on rain-slick cobblestones, the echo of old betrayals. But now Mariel's touch is here, grounding him.

"I was wrong," Lucien whispers. "All this time, I thought distance could keep you safe. But standing alone made us targets." He exhales, voice scraping raw. "You see me, Mariel. Not the man I pretend to be. The man I am, scars and all."

She doesn't flinch.

"Good," Mariel breathes, squeezing his fingers. "Because the man you are is the one I choose—every time. I'm scared for you. For us. But hiding doesn't protect anything. It just lets the threat dictate the rules."

They trade pens, wordlessly synchronizing a rhythm that has belonged only to crisis and confession. Mariel tilts her head, curiosity warming her gaze. "What if the future they want for us—splintered, fearful—isn't the only outcome? What if the real risk is not trusting our partnership enough?"

Lucien half-smiles, faint and fragile. "Then let's make the rules ourselves."

She lets out a soft breath, almost laughter. Her palm lingers over his heart, feeling its frantic pace slow. "Then we set the trap together. We defend together. Agreed?"

He nods. The vulnerability in his eyes is a confession, brighter than any promise he has ever spoken.

Lucien moves to the wall safe behind an antique globe—faint lavender scent from Mariel's cooling tea filling the room as the safe clicks open. He withdraws a midnight-black drive, cool as river stone, and hands it to her. "My private archives. Everything I've held back—from everyone. If something happens, you'll have what's needed... to defend, to destroy, to survive."

Mariel accepts the drive with both hands, solemn. "You trust me with everything?"

"You've trusted me with yourself," Lucien answers. "Now I finally deserve it."

Mariel's fingers fly across her tablet, activating the lockdown protocol. Electric locks seal, smart glass shades tint, and the faint crackle of laser grids fills the silence. They're safe—together, or as close to it as the world allows.

Lucien steps beside Mariel at the window. The city breathes neon and haze below. He watches her profile, the way fierce resolve and tenderness battle on her face, and lets the last walls between them slip.

Outside, night is gathering. Most would call it an omen. For them, it's challenge and vow. They face the darkness at the glass, two silhouettes braced for whatever storm will come—knowing this time, neither will face it alone.

Rain's Discovery

A faint, antiseptic glow bathes Darius's private office, the only resistance to midnight's encroaching dark. Cream-colored walls blur under the low wash of amber from his desk lamp, masked further by the ivy-shadowed window, where city lights glint like distant, unspeaking witnesses. The quiet is textured—barely disturbed by the subtle whir of climate control and the ceaseless, muffled beep of a distant heart monitor somewhere deeper in the hospital. On his polished oak desk, a series of screens flicker, each displaying pieces of a world unraveling at its seams.

Darius sits with his back rigid, shoulders squared beneath the tailored cut of his suit, his fingers moving in deliberate, near-soundless patterns across encrypted logins and biometric verifications. The dimness accentuates the lines of exhaustion on his face; the scar on his forearm, vivid in this light, seems a fresh reminder rather than a distant history. The air tastes of recycled air and old coffee—a trace of anxiety layered beneath professionalism.

He calls up the latest surveillance folder: a mosaic of grainy footage, time-stamped, labeled by site and severity. His gaze snags on a video frame—a saboteur's gloved hand, paused mid-motion in a pool of spilled coolant. Framed in that frozen second, there's a painted mark: a serpent, black and coiling, fangs bared, entwined with the thin blade of a dagger. Darius's breath catches. He enlarges the frame, heart stilled in a slow, cold drum. His eyes narrow, seeing not just a logo, but a threat sharpened into myth.

On another screen, threads of intercepted emails unravel. Once, their encryption would have seemed impenetrable. Now, patterns emerge. The same symbol—digital, stylized, tucked among false headers and random noise—curls its way into subject lines or footers, imprinted like an unbreakable sigil. The scent of burnt silicon seems to linger, a phantom born of too many hours at war with codes and intentions.

He runs comparison queries, fingers now taut. Old reports flood the printer: timestamps of coordinated attacks on Brotherhood properties, from fires that licked the marble portico of Caius's headquarters to the quiet, silent sabotage of a research lab's generator. Darius overlays the serpent and dagger symbol, draws red lines from the first artifact to the most recent, mapping moments when their world wobbled beneath hidden intrusion.

Each strike is no longer an isolated spark in the dark. The pattern burns hot and logical—a campaign waged in calculated increments. The Brotherhood, once untouchable, is being whittled down by an adversary who understands both spectacle and silence. The realization is a vise, squeezing the air from his chest, yet his mind sharpens around it. These are not random ghosts—they are the servants of something larger, ancient in ambition, tireless in its complexity.

A faint taste of bitterness creeps up his throat. Vulnerability pervades this place now, he thinks; the Brotherhood's sanctuaries—once fortresses—are being mapped, stalked, punctured with impunity. Every burned archive, hacked system, vanished courier is a tremor in the city's carefully balanced order. The secret war raging beneath marble and glass has begun to seep through, threatening not only power, but the myth of control binding the city's elite. The politics of privilege tremble in the shadow cast by unseen hands. If the Brotherhood falters, the city's constellation of alliances will fracture, and the old rules—unwritten but merciless—will yield to something new, less human, more ruthless.

Darius presses his knuckles against his jaw, feeling both the familiar grind of frustration and, in the space beneath, a flickering surge of hope. The puzzle unfolds beneath his hands—its very existence a sign that their enemy, for all their caution, can be seen.

He speed-dials Lila. The line rings only once.

"Darius?" Her voice is softer than the city beyond, but there's a tension, a readiness he has grown to depend on.

"I need you here. Now. There's something you have to see," he says, urgency cutting through his even tone.

"I'm on my way. Ten minutes."

She appears, silhouetted in the frame of the door. She moves toward him, hair pulled back, focus absolute. Darius gestures to the printouts already spreading like fractured wings across the desk and up the wall.

"Look at this," he says, tapping the serpent-dagger symbol. "It's not just on tonight's footage. Cross-reference it to the intrusions last quarter—here, and here. And in the intercepted emails—every attack, every message, marked by the same thing."

Lila studies the evidence, the dim light reflecting in her serious eyes. "Who leaves a signature unless they want it found? Or they're arrogant enough to think we'll never connect it," she murmurs, tracing the web of lines between dots on the city map.

"Or they want us to know the shape of the monster we're up against," Darius replies, his voice low.

They don't speak for a while, the silence thickening as realization sets in. On the wall, red lines converge, a constellation of violence and coded warnings.

Darius plants his palm on the desk, jaw tight. "This isn't a rival playing for shares. It's a society—hidden, ancient, organized. And they want us to see their work."

They stand shoulder to shoulder, gazes fixed on the spreading network of evidence. In that charged quiet, the next move is both invitation and warning—one step closer to war, each heartbeat counting down to the city's next reckoning.

The study's door thuds softly closed behind Lila, sealing off the predawn hush of the fortified residence. Shadows cluster against the book-lined walls, broken only by the glow from the desk lamp where Darius sits hunched, his face carved with lines of fatigue. The air is thick with coffee, fraying nerves, and the faint metallic scent of warmed circuitry. Lila crosses the wool rug in bare feet, feeling grit from the outside world clinging to her skin—remnants of hours spent running interference on disaster. She silently takes her place beside him, their shoulders brushing, a triangle of lamplight trapping both their reflections in the monitor's sheen.

Outside, the city's hush is unnatural, the usual distant throb of ambulances and construction blotted out by soundproof glass and the thick silence that means the world is holding its breath. Darius zooms in on the cipher again, digits tumbling in dizzying permutations. Lila smooths a loose strand of hair behind her ear, eyes flicking across the scrolling streams. She sketches quick, slanted notations on a yellow legal pad, her handwriting growing sharp and angular with every new pattern.

"Sixth message," Darius murmurs, voice still hoarse from lack of sleep. "This string—see the double sixes?"

Lila leans in, warmth brushing his arm. "Coordinates, maybe. Add the time stamp to the previous IP ping. Look—there's the city grid reference. That's..." She trails off, heart jerking as she matches the code to a street they both know—a Brotherhood drop-off site razed only a week ago, smoke still lingering in her memory. Her hand trembles faintly as she points out the overlap.

Darius's proximity grounds her; she breathes in the faint scent of his aftershave and sweat and the old paper that always clings to his shirt. The silence between them is taut, electric, not empty at all.

"I'll cross-check it," he says, already opening another encrypted portal. Keystrokes tick rapid-fire beneath his fingertips. Lila listens for the underlying rhythm, lets it steady her. She feels how much she needs that steadiness now.

She draws in a shaky breath. The urge to curl into herself—bury her head, close her eyes, let someone else shoulder this responsibility—flickers and dies with each practiced movement of her pen. Instead, she swivels to the second laptop, opening spreadsheets laced with arcane names and offshore codes.

Her mind whirls through memories: the taste of brine and blood the night her brother vanished, the hush of her mother weeping behind a closed bathroom door, the relentless pressure to keep family safe no matter the personal cost. The world of the Brotherhood always seemed vast, untouchable, but now she tastes its fragility on her tongue with every cryptic message. She is not allowed to fail—not again.

"Wait," Darius says. "The Cayman conduit just lit up." He draws her gaze with a single tilt of the screen, revealing an account number already infamous from weeks of financial sleuthing. "Four transfers, three within the last forty-eight hours."

"All routed through shell listings. And look—" Lila's finger hovers above another column, "—recipients match the aliases in those missing visitor logs at the secondary wing." She glances at Darius, catches the glint of recognition in his eyes.

A silent agreement forms—no fear, not here. Instead, bare-knuckled resolve. Lila clamps down her exhaustion, draws strength from Darius's unwavering focus, his presence a stubborn counterweight to her own lapses of hope.

Darius sorts through cold, hard numbers; Lila pulls background reports from an accordion file, ink already smudged from long hours. She sorts the faces, the neat biographies of power and privilege—one by one, notes hinge on discrepancies: a political consultant with mysterious janitorial clearance; a businessman with security tags issued for just a single midnight hour.

The patterns reveal themselves, dark threads drawing toward the city's heart.

Lila taps her notepad with growing urgency. "None of this is accidental. These clearances—there's a gatekeeper, somewhere inside our system. They're letting the fox in every time."

Darius looks up, jaw clenched but eyes gentler than they were at midnight. "And we're standing on the wrong side of the door."

She swallows hard. His words strike deeper than accusation, echoing old wounds she never let heal. Again, failure feels close.

"But we see it now," she presses, her voice rough—willing herself not to flinch. "It's numbers, names, real places—real people. We can use that."

His hand finds hers, fingers curling over her knuckles. "We will. We always do."

Glass clinks softly as Lila reaches behind her for another printout. Darius projects the digital maps onto the far wall; their colors carve up the shadows. The network is sprawling—arteries of data tie safehouses to unnamed owners, bank accounts to men and women who slip between boardrooms like ghosts. Red arcs stretch in widening circles, lines drawn with a trembling marker. The city bleeds out under their gaze.

She pins the last printout to the corkboard, tapping a profile with a distinctive coding signature—a flourish only an arrogant hacker would use if they thought they'd never be found.

Darius circles the farthest node on the map, marker squealing beneath the pressure, sweat misting his brow. "It's worse than we thought. If we don't stop this, they'll hit everything at once." His voice is ragged, and she hears in it both warning and promise—a stake pressed deep beneath bone.

As the early light begins to seep beneath the curtains, they stand back, hands clasped, and stare at the tangled web that binds them. Time is running out.

Dawn hasn't touched the sky yet, but the fortified safe house glows with cold, artificial light—a place carved from bedrock and paranoia, far from city eyes and ears. Thick steel doors insulate against the chill and the world beyond, while the stale scent of concrete mingles with a metallic tang—gun oil, maybe, or the tang of nerves. Inside, tension vibrates through the air, alive in restless footsteps and clipped whispers as the five couples file into the council chamber.

Darius stands at the head of the round table, evidence folders arranged like a ritual before him. The emblem of the Orion constellation glimmers beneath their hands—etched into blackened oak by men who once trusted each other without question. That trust feels thin now, stretched across shadows and secrets. Darius clears his throat, the click of the outdated projector echoing in the hush as encrypted files bloom across the wall—serpents coiling around daggers, trails of shell corporations, and time-stamped warnings.

He speaks in an even tone, every detail measured, as laser pointers sweep over coded symbols, grainy surveillance stills, and flowcharts exposing the pattern of infiltration. "They have insiders. Patterns hidden in digital traffic," he says. "Funds routed through shadows, timed with our every vulnerability. This isn't petty sabotage—it's systemic, orchestrated."

A low hiss escapes Silas, arms folded, eyes needle-sharp. Lucien leans forward, jaw clenched, gaze flicking from dossier to projected accounts. "If we have rats, how do we poison their nest? We vet our own, or we're walking blind."

Caius's voice cuts in, hard and edged by sleeplessness. "How deep does this spiral go, Darius? Are we already breached at the core, or is this noise to keep us paranoid?"

Orion paces the perimeter, fists balled, his muttering almost lost beneath the thrumming security locks. "Every time I think we patch one hole, another one tears open. Are we chasing phantoms, or has someone marked us for extinction?"

Across the table, the women exchange glances threaded with questions and fear. Seraphina watches Caius with an unblinking steadiness,

Mariel traces the edge of a printout, lips pursed; Elara reaches beneath the table, seeking Orion's hand, while Lila's eyes dart between pages and faces with restless calculation. Hana sits serene, but her fingers flex—seeking an anchor, or perhaps readying to fight.

"Enough second-guessing," Lucien snaps. "If we fracture here, we're as good as dead." He pushes a file to Silas. "We build new digital countermeasures. No more legacy lines, no familiar routines. I'll audit the net myself."

Silas nods, but his silence says more than agreement. "And every political link, every compromised contact—we rip them from the root. I'll take point there. No more ghosts moving through locked doors."

Lila slides a sheet across to Darius, voice soft but unyielding. "We'll need an internal chain. Secure, analog if we must. Face-to-face for all critical alerts."

Seraphina leans in, her voice burning low. "And what about us? They target from the inside. If we turn our backs even for a second—"

Mariel interrupts, her tone cool and precise. "Then we set the trap. Make them show themselves. No one moves alone. Not anymore."

The group divides along these new lines—surveillance, countermeasure, security, and escape. Each couple falls into a rhythm born of hard-won trust and necessity, voices overlapping, the air charged with urgency and a brittle hope.

"We're not just protecting assets," Darius intones quietly, "we're protecting each other. If we fail, the fallout swallows more than empires. It takes families." His eyes meet Lila's—a silent vow passing between them.

Caius gathers their attention, his presence a dark star drawing the room's orbit. "We stand, or we shatter. There's no middle ground. We pledged our blood to the same constellation. Don't forget what that costs. Or what it means. We win together. Or not at all."

They fall silent, the gravity of the words settling around them. Suspicion still flickers—caught in sideward glances, in the measured way Seraphina squeezes Caius's hand, in the wariness with which Hana studies the lines of the table. Loyalties feel fragile, tested by the knowledge that any of them could be the breach.

Darius feels the weight rooting deep in his bones—responsibility scraping raw at logic and heart alike. He sees how exhaustion has hollowed out Lucien's bravado, how Silas's solitude is starting to crack. He senses the cost pressing in on their partners—women who have risked everything for love and now must gamble on faith in a system with more fractures than seams.

They rise—hands finding the emblem at the table's heart, skin on cold wood traced with cosmic lines. One by one, voices speak, low and hoarse or strong and steady: "Together." "We fight." "They won't find us unprepared."

The vow rings through the chamber—sacred, or maybe desperate. And outside, morning leaves the city still cloaked in dark. The war against the unseen has only just begun.

Storm's Collapse

The hush in the east corridor of Orion's estate is thick—a pause heavy with the taste of scorched metal and fear, not so much silence as the sharp-edged aftermath of violence. The marble underfoot bears the memory of hurried boots and spilled secrets. Cold air curls in from cracks around high windows, mixing the scents of ozone, stress sweat, and the faint citrus polish used hours earlier by staff who now tremble in locked rooms. The entire house vibrates with the uneasy echo of the attack that has just broken across the Brotherhood's defenses, as if the world itself had gone brittle.

Nova slinks out first—her frame low, spine a quivering bow. Claws scrabble desperately on the glassy surface, each tap as loud as a gunshot. The corridor is dim, lit only by the failed promise of sconces gutted to their embers, the darkness speckled with faint blue glimmers from security panels. Nova's eyes, wild and wide, flicker with a primal warning Orion has learned to trust. She darts from a half-open service door, coat bristling, teeth clacking in the raw hush.

A shape uncoils from the shadow. The intruder's mask is impersonal and smooth—black fabric, faceless, eyes little more than pits of shadow. Gloves flex, measured and certain. A ripple of muscle beneath tailored black hints at training, not panic. One swift, chillingly precise movement, and Nova is trapped—cornered against the cold wall by a body with a menace the estate's high walls were built to keep out. Breath steams in shallow bursts as Nova cowers back, a low, strangled snarl trembling out of her, halfway between rage and terror.

Orion tears onto the scene, feet slamming against the marble with reckless speed that barely avoids a fall. He skids, knees locked tight, the adrenaline roar in his skull drowning out everything but Nova's snarl—familiar, searing through old wounds. "Nova!" His voice cracks, knotted with fear, warping the tranquil hush into chaos. He crashes into the intruder with all the force of a landslide, shoulder first, hands a blur of clenched fury. The masked figure gives ground, surprise visible in the twitch of arms as Orion pries him off Nova.

For a heartbeat, there's a tangle—scrabbling limbs, a scuff of boot striking glass. Orion doesn't feel the pain when his knuckles split open on the intruder's shoulder, doesn't register the warmth of blood. He only knows heat, the burn of breath gone raw. The man wriggles free with unnatural agility, ducking under Orion's wild swing, and hurls himself through the nearest window. The glass shrieks—a shattering gash that unleashes winter air and panic's aftertaste. A vase topples from the ledge and explodes, ceramic shards leaping across the marble.

Orion collapses, knees hitting the ground hard—he doesn't bother to rise, can't. He claws Nova to him, fingers so frantic they barely register the silk of her coat, searching every inch for blood, a wound, anything. Nova whines softly, but there's no red—only wild panting, only the damp heat of her muzzle pressed to Orion's collarbone. His hands shake. His vision blurs, and fury surges—a tornado crashing against his ribcage and skull as helplessness curdles into violence. He hurls the nearest thing—an antique vase—across the corridor, the sound splintering the haunted hush.

The estate is an animal, wounded and wary, every sensor alive, every heartbeat on edge. Orion's mind spins, torn backward. Not again—not her. He remembers another night—gunfire outside, Nova screaming, bloody pawprints smeared across polished terrazzo. That memory lives in him with a parasite's persistence, colors every footstep when danger stirs, whispers what he has to lose.

Tonight should have been safe. The Brotherhood regrouped after the recent strike, every system checked, every alarm doubled. The world outside, boiling with threat, was supposed to be held at bay by glass, steel, and trust in the walls he built. But fear slips through cracks, always. Old wounds, jagged and hungry, gape wider—he's never fast enough. His recklessness, his refusal to lock down, to let someone else protect for once—every impulse feels like a nail hammered through the future.

Is this how it ends? His hands, capable of shielding an empire, can't even keep this single soul safe. The dull iron taste of self-loathing thickens in his mouth. Helplessness settles on his shoulders. Nova's weight in his arms feels both a relief and a confession—if he'd been slower, if luck had tipped wrong, she'd be gone. He's made promises to her, to Elara, to the Brotherhood—with each one, the price of failure grows. Tonight the estate is bright with panic, and Orion's guilt is the sharpest cut of all.

Nova shivers in his lap, pressing into him until his chest aches. He buries his face in her fur, breath hitching, curses forced between clenched teeth. Weakness: it stings. The corridor is littered with white shards and dark streaks of blood from his knuckles. The only living warmth he can claim is Nova, silent now, eyes twin moons fixed on his face. Orion lets himself break—just for these seconds—his sobs ragged, torn straight from buried places he pretends don't exist. The house watches. Shadows gather. Somewhere, an alarm wails, but he can't move. Blood stains his hands. Nova nestles closer, the only proof that tonight, at least, he did not lose everything.

The doors to Orion's private sitting room are locked, an impenetrable barrier against the chaos muttering in the halls. Thick velvet curtains swallow the world, letting only the stain of weak amber lamplight puddle across the floorboards. Shadows cling to the edges—not the sharp kind, but the uncertain, haunted ones that linger after violence. In the hush, Nova's breath sounds almost human: a broken rhythm, trembling, occasionally shuddering.

Orion sits cross-legged on the plush rug, his back pressed to the wall, Nova's silken warmth pressed tightly against his chest. His eyes are the wrong kind of red, bloodshot and rimmed with shadows, his jaw locked so hard that a muscle pulses beneath mottled skin. Every tendon in his hand quivers, still marked with the pattern of teeth and glass. The estate's silence is a strained thing, heavy and waiting.

Elara doesn't hesitate at the threshold—she folds herself softly to the rug beside him, not reaching, not demanding. Her presence glides into the shattered quiet, filling the air with the scent of lavender and rain-drenched stone. Orion does not speak. His breath comes in shallow drafts, cut with the occasional rasp of a desperate swallow.

She waits, hands folded in her lap, letting her heartbeat anchor her to the moment. The cold from the floor creeps through the silk of her dress, grounding her further. There's no judgment in her eyes as she regards him—only a fierce, unwavering calm, steady as bedrock. She knows better than to pierce silence with empty comfort.

Minutes crawl by, measured only by the delicate tremors that shiver through Orion's body, reverberating against Nova's anxious huff. Elara's gaze falls on his hands—so strong, now useless, stained crimson. A surge of protectiveness sweeps up from her gut; she draws a slow, deliberate breath, bracing herself before she moves.

Her touch is gentle but sure as she finds Orion's trembling hand, sliding her palm into his and squeezing. His fingers twitch as if electrified, then tighten against hers as if to test her solidity. She leans closer, meeting his shattered gaze, her thumb stroking over the rough scab forming along his knuckles.

"Breathe with me," she urges, her voice a low hum in the dark. "You've walked through hell before, Orion. I know you. You're not alone—not tonight, not ever."

Orion's mouth works, shaped by fury and grief in equal measure, but no words find their way out. His stare falls to their entwined fingers, as if witnessing something rare and precious—something still intact. He blinks, breathing ragged. The trembling subsides, just a fraction.

Elara's free hand comes up, brushing the locks of hair clinging damp to his forehead. Her fingers cradle his jaw. She traces away the streaks under his eyes with the pads of her thumbs, the touch firm, grounding. She presses closer, her knees touching his, her heartbeat as steady as a metronome. His hand darts up, gripping her wrist, desperate for a tether.

"Look at me," she whispers, and waits until his gaze rises again. "I won't let you drown in this. Whatever you're seeing—whatever you're blaming yourself for—you held Nova safe. You brought her back."

He shudders, his grip convulsing once more.

"If you think you failed," she breathes right against his temple, "then let me be your strength tonight. I will stand between you and that guilt as long as it takes."

Something in Orion's tight frame crumples. He draws in a breath, salty with grief, then lets it out—slow, unsteady, but loosed from the edge of panic. He buries his forehead into her shoulder, his voice muffled but rough.

"I nearly let it happen again, Elara. I can't—"

"You didn't," she cuts in, still gentle but steel-edged. "Nova is here. You are here. That's enough for now."

Her lips brush his ear as she urges him to breathe, again and again, letting the steadiness of her own ribcage guide his fractured rhythm.

He slumps forward, the fight gone from his body, pressed full weight into her. For a heartbeat, there is only the shared hush of broken survivors and the sound of Nova's relieved sigh as the dog—no, family—crawls into Elara's lap, nose nudging her palm.

"I can't lose either of you," Orion says, voice cracked and raw.

She wraps both arms around him, letting his anguish settle against her. "You won't," she promises. "Not while I stand."

He nods against her, silent. In that cocoon—curtains drawn, lamp flickering, the storm outside held at bay—something shifts. Orion lets her strength anchor him, lets their grief and hope mingle. For the first time since the attack, his breath begins to steady, their heartbeats syncing in the darkness.

Nova sighs once, a warm shape pressed between them—a living affirmation. Orion's next breath shudders quieter still, gratitude woven through it.

"Thank you," he whispers—a vow, a plea, a lifeline—and the three of them remain, suspended in fragile, necessary peace, as the house finally dares to rest.

They sit close on the sunroom's suede sofa, the air in the estate still heavy, as if the walls themselves remember. Nova's body forms a tight circle at their feet, her chest rising and falling, each breath steadying Orion's own. He's hunched forward, elbows digging into his thighs, knuckles scraped raw and stained. Morning's first light is just beginning to slip past the thick glass, brushing their tangled shadows across the amber floor. A scent lingers—coffee grown cold, ozone from shattered glass, a faint trace of Nova's fear and sweat clinging to Orion's shirt.

Orion's throat aches when he forces sound out. "I keep thinking I'd have lost her if I'd been three seconds slower. Always nearly losing her. Or you. I hate that I can't—" His voice cracks, rough as gravel. "They keep slipping through my hands." He squeezes his temples, jaw clamped hard enough to ache.

Elara leans in, her thigh pressing to his—solid, warm. The world feels real again when she's this close. Her hands cover his, skin gentle and unyielding. "You didn't lose her, Orion. And you won't lose me, either. I'm scared too." She gives his hands a subtle squeeze, grounding him in the now. "But if we let fear or guilt hollow us out, they win. If you lock yourself away, I can't reach you. And I need you beside me. I can only fight for you—we can only win—if we do it together."

He looks at her—really looks. There's an honesty in her vulnerability, in the tremor hidden beneath her even tone. He listens. The estate feels unnaturally still, as if the hush between heartbeats holds them suspended: survivor and anchor, storm and shelter.

Orion's skin tingles with memory. He's seen this before—the way security can buckle and fate slip through cracks no matter how tightly he tries to seal them. Years ago, after another midnight—different intruder, different room—he'd raced Nova to an emergency vet, blood streaked through her fur. There was the hospital siege, the moment he toppled a man twice his size for threatening Elara. Despite all his force and strategy, the world always found a new weak spot—an unlocked door, a trusted staff member gone rogue, the echo of betrayal from someone once called brother. The Brotherhood's power was supposed to be unbreakable, but in practice, it's a lattice riddled with invisible fractures—only held steady by relentless vigilance, instinct, and love's desperate inventiveness.

He'd built his reputation on control—the ability to command, to take hits and strike back, to weather any assault. But the more he's bled, the more he's realized that control is an illusion that shatters at three a.m. under the knife's glint or a scream that comes too late. These wounds have changed him. Hardened some core inside, but left fissures where guilt and anger fester. He hates the wildness in him—the way his own rage nearly scared Elara tonight. But he hates most the sense that no matter what he does, the people he loves will always be caught in the crossfire of his failures.

The thought of that loss—the empty house, Nova's too-small shadow gone, Elara's voice silent—claws at his chest. But there's Elara now, steadying his pulse, inviting him to keep breathing, to build something stronger from the ruins.

"Security is failing," Orion says finally. "I want every person on this property re-vetted. Double the guard rotations—inside, not just at the gate. Every animal, every family member, under watch. Hell, I want sensors on windows. No more blind spots."

Elara meets his fire with her own quiet resolve. "It's time for a complete review of staff—no assumptions. I'll draft protocols tonight—silent alarms, scanning entry logs, rotation of duties. We can't just react to threats anymore. We have to expect them. I'll oversee it myself."

He nods, a thread of relief weaving through the tension. "Together, E. Not just my rules, yours too. Partners." He touches her cheek, voice raw but steadier. "The only thing that snapped me back tonight was you. I'd have drowned if you hadn't been here."

She touches his scarred jaw, thumb lingering. "You pulled yourself back, but I stood beside you. That's what we do—weather the darkness and the storm. Shoulder to shoulder. I'm not letting go."

He pulls her close, arms anchoring her—his fortress, but she is the steel that holds the walls. He breathes in her scent: wild jasmine, sweat, the faintest trace of clean linen, banishing blood and terror from his mind. Nova, sensing the peace shifting, climbs into Elara's lap, pressing her cold nose into Orion's wrist—a small, vital circle of trust still unbroken.

For a long moment, the dawn becomes their covenant. Orion presses his forehead to Elara's, both eyes open now and seeing the same horizon. "We face them together. Whatever comes. Whatever it costs."

Voices and footsteps echo distantly—Brotherhood regrouping, the world outside sharpening. But inside this sunlit hush, they make their vow, unyielding—three heartbeats, one promise, dawn's light flickering gold on scars that will not break.

Ashes to Ashes

Night drapes itself over Silas's private office, heavy and silent. The staccato tap of rain against the fractured window is a quiet percussion, the scent of petrichor and ozone drifting up through a gap in the glass. Once, the gleam of this place reflected an impenetrable power—white marble, sharp chrome, the subtle perfume of expensive paper and ink. Now, cracks spiderweb across the pane, transforming the city lights into broken constellations. The overhead fluorescents flicker, lending a wavering translucence to shadows that have become too comfortable here.

Silas sits alone behind his desk, hunched, a silhouette carved from fatigue and unrest. The desk is a chaos of intercepted communiqués and encrypted files, each one marked by his steady hand, evidence of nights spent chasing whispers through labyrinths of code and deceit. In the hush, the soft hum of his computer is both a lifeline and a curse. He scrolls, eyes scanning lines of symbols blooming into meaning for him alone—phrases buried in innocuous correspondence, subtle enough to pass as noise. But the secrets spill themselves neatly, damningly: site access points, shipment manifest edits, timing that syncs too precisely to be random.

He lifts his gaze to a wall-mounted board mapped with colored pins and curling threads. Red for breaches. Blue for unexplained delays. Gold for the rare victories where their defenses held. His hand hovers, trembling now, then pins another crimson mark—tonight's attack, logged at a time that matches a message timestamped with chilling precision. The pattern emerges, undeniable, as if the betrayal wishes to be seen at last. A cold sweat breaks on his skin.

He leans over, staring at his reflection in the lustrous ebony of the desk: hard, angular features; the scar on his jaw stark and pale tonight. He considers how easily secrets erode trust, how his own obsessive need for control, for hiding the truest parts of himself, built walls within the Brotherhood as much as around it. Always, he imagined that secrecy would keep them safe—keep Hana safe—but it only sharpened the blade that now hovers over them all, wielded by someone who wore a brother's face.

He stifles a shudder, desperation flickering in his fingers as he types commands to cross-reference dates and routes. Each outcome is more conclusive, yet the implication sinks deep, as abrasive as glass dust in the lungs. Could it have been different if he'd set aside pride and let them in sooner? He tries to summon the memory of the Brotherhood forming, back when they swore their oaths under starlit silence, each man's hand steady. He remembers the quiet certainty, the unspoken conviction that unity was armor. But unity was always a mask, hiding rifts that time has only widened.

A scraping sound; his German Shepherd, Raven, slips through the open door and settles at his feet with a low, comforting huff. Fur brushes against Silas's ankle, grounding him amid the tension.

"Raven," Silas breaks the silence, his voice so low it nearly drowns in the throb of distant thunder. "Too late for walks. Too late for second chances."

He places the final pin, then opens a secure folder on his desktop. The printer whirs awake, churning out the critical evidence—a tangible weight he gathers with shaking hands. He tucks the documents into a black portfolio and snaps the lock shut with a practiced, almost ritualistic click. He slips the portfolio into a battered briefcase, fingers lingering on the clasp as if searching for some final reassurance. The cool metal is slick against sweat-damp skin, subtly catching the city's refracted glow.

For a breath, he stands, pressing his palms flat against the glass as rain streaks its surface. Below, the city simmers—cars drifting through wet streets, neon pulsing, shadows shifting in alleys that have swallowed so many secrets. If he could tear back the layers, glimpse the world as it truly is, would it undo the ruin now gnawing at everything he's loved and led?

He is a keeper of silence, shaped by the old upheavals where secrecy was survival and trust a calculated risk. There were times he ignored quieter alarms—the look in Caius's eyes during their first fallout; the cautious tension in Darius's handshake after an early betrayal; the way Hana's voice would soften, asking what burdens he kept from sight. Always, he circled the perimeter, locking away everything vital, haunted by the certainty that to reveal weakness meant inviting destruction.

Now that choice feels like a curse. All his efforts to shield the Brotherhood, his refusal to show the jagged fear within, have left them open for one of their own to slip a knife through their defenses. Each betrayal unspools not just tonight's disaster, but every suppressed doubt and unspoken apology.

For a moment, he wishes for Hana's touch—her calm, her unwavering faith. But this night is solitude, and he must be both judge and witness in the court of his failures.

Lightning flashes, illuminating the deep fissures in the glass and his own haunted reflection. Grief and fury knot in his chest. Into this fractured mirror, the truth stares back—he cannot carry this alone anymore.

He turns from the pane, every muscle taut, and fastens the briefcase shut one final time, resolve steeling in his eyes. The city pulses beneath him—a world built on secrets, now forever changed.

The secure conference room hums with the low pulse of the Brotherhood's defenses—steel doors sealed, amber sconces flaring just enough to chase away shadows from the circular granite walls. At its center, the towering table glows beneath projected constellations, polished leather chairs drawn in a tense arc. Silas stands at one end, shoulders squared beneath his crisp suit, but his eyes are lined with fatigue, the folder clutched in knuckle-whitened hands. For a moment, the only sounds are the tick of a distant clock and the tap of his shoes on stone.

The others file in, drawn by his message—Caius's presence like a thundercloud barely held in check, Lucien silent and sharp-eyed, Darius moving with the distraction of a man pulled from a living nightmare. Orion is the last to arrive, jaw set, fists balled as if the very air has betrayed him. Their partners assemble at their sides: Seraphina's gaze is fierce and searching, Mariel slips a slim tablet from her bag, Lila's hand immediately finding Darius's, and Elara places herself between Orion's twitching hands and the table's edge.

Silas steps forward, his voice grinding through the silence. "We have a problem deeper than attacks from the outside. The evidence is here." He slides the sleek folder across the table; its surface gleams like oil, slick with secrets. With deliberate care, he lays out the evidence—printed messages, photographs, timestamps, charts now projected across the immense wall screens, the blue-white light flickering across faces set in stone.

Caius leans forward, his features chiseling even sharper. "You're saying one of us..." His words trail, crushed under the weight of implication.

Lucien's words cut in, precise as scalpels. "Show the timestamps. What else do we have besides speculation? Patterns can be drawn in spilled wine if you wish it badly enough."

Darius drops into his chair, pale beneath the olive tint of his skin, free hand trembling on his thigh as he reads the lines of communications—each one a scar carved into their trust. Lila squeezes his hand gently, grounding him, thumb brushing comfort into his skin like balm. Orion's boots scrape restlessly against the floor, contained violence in every sinew. Elara places her palm on his arm, a grounding pressure, and he stills with great effort, eyes flashing beneath storm-dark lashes.

Silas's mouth is dry, tongue thick with dread. He finds his voice only by necessity. "Everything lines up. The codes used... the specific knowledge. The saboteur is here—always has been." His own words ring in his ears like a curse, guilt souring the back of his throat, the iron-cold taste of failure. He sees Hana's eyes—steady, unwavering—meeting his when he falters, but the knot in his gut only tightens further.

"You're certain?" Seraphina's words are a blade, quick and bright. "How could this happen under our noses, Silas? Has everything we built always stood on rotting ground?"

Mariel's stylus glides over the illuminated screen, her face impassive save for the slight bite of her lip. She avoids Caius's searching glare, lips pressed thin as she records, eyes darting between the names and dates. Lila's fingers tremble in Darius's grasp, her eyes wet but not yet spilling over. In one corner, Elara watches every movement, reading the language of shoulders and eyes, quietly gathering what holds and what frays.

A current whips through the room—fear, suspicion, the old rivalry between Caius and Lucien rising just beneath their voices. Lucien's gaze narrows, searching for cracks in what's presented. "There's a gap—right here, between when the server notifications hit and when the response came." He points, voice a quiet accusation. "Why wasn't this seen until now?"

Silas bites down, breath short as he answers. "Because... I was too focused on hunting predators at the gates. I didn't look inward. I—" His voice cracks, shame slipping through his defenses. "I should have seen this sooner." He steels himself, feels Hana's presence behind him—a silent plea not to dissolve into regret.

"Someone's hiding. Someone we trusted." Orion's voice is ragged, barely more than a growl. "I want answers—I want names. Who's been feeding us to the wolves?"

Seraphina lashes back, "Don't act like we're all suspects. If you were so sure, Silas, why bring us together blind?" Her accusation isn't just for him—she looks around, challenging any of them to admit guilt.

Lucien shakes his head, voice cool. "This isn't theater. If there's a traitor, we'll find them. But now's not the moment to turn on each other out of panic."

Darius looks up, hollow-eyed. "Then what do we do? Who can we trust if not ourselves?"

A hush stretches, thick and cloying. Each pair recoils slightly from the others—shoulders close, but hearts barricaded. Shared history, once a lifeline, now feels like a trap sprung shut. Alliances shift in silent glances: wary, testing, hesitant to reforge the bonds now charred by doubt. No one dares move first, as if a wrong word might shatter the remnants of faith they cling to.

Caius breaks the stillness, his fist smashing down with a thunderous crack against the oak. "We are not undone by this—not by poison or by shadows." But his voice, though defiant, quavers—betraying a fracture as raw as any wound, echoing off the room's stone heart.

The meeting room feels like a pressure cooker about to blow, all the oxygen thick with suspicion and sour with the scent of coffee gone cold. Every face is raw, shadowed by the blue static from the wall screens still pulsing with evidence. Caius's fist is clenched on the table, Lucien's gaze razor-sharp, Darius sitting stiff and pale beside Lila, Orion straining at the end of the long arc of light, jaw tense, Elara's hand steady on his wrist. The partners linger near, forming a barrier of solidarity and nerves. Eyes dart. Throats clear. The silence is brittle as spun glass.

Then Hana rises, her movement subtle but unmissable, the gentle hush of her chair legs against the marble a small anchor in the turbulent sea. Her frame is not large, but she stands with a kind of quiet gravity, eyes clear and unwavering.

"We have faced far worse than this alone," she says, her voice soft, warming the cold steel and stone of the room. "But we survived because we faced it together. We made an oath—one that wasn't just words." She lets her gaze pass around the ring: old wounds gleam there, the half-remembered glint of hope and cost. "And we endured. Betrayal is what our enemies want for us, not what we are."

Her words settle into the silence, cutting through the panic—soft, but iron-strong.

Hana crosses the room's charged space to Silas, whose shoulders are drawn so tight they barely move with his breath. She lays her palm on his forearm. The gesture is unhurried—no trembling, no apology. Her fingers press not in comfort, but in solidarity, grounding.

"Silas. You saw what none of us wanted to see. That took more strength than any secret," she tells him, her tone a gentle, resonant chord only he can truly hear. "You're not weak for feeling what you do. Lead us with that courage. Not guilt. We need you whole."

Silas turns his head—the faint light catches the edge of old scars and newer lines of fatigue. There is gratitude in his eyes, the kind that's raw and unguarded, and something else too: belief, stitched back together where it nearly ripped.

Hana doesn't let go. She lifts her eyes to the others, the heat in her gaze steady as a forge. "None of us can afford to turn on each other. Not now. The true traitor—whoever it is—feeds on doubt. That's their weapon. Ours has always been unity. Trust may feel impossible. But without it, we have already lost more than any cipher or fortune."

The couples shift closer. Lila's grip on Darius softens; Mariel's pen is forgotten; Elara's arm tightens around Orion's frame, coaxing him to stillness. Caius's composure regains a hard edge, and Seraphina's expression flickers—a touch of guilt, then gratitude.

"It's what we built from," Hana continues. "Every scar. Every loss. We became more than what was done to us." Her gaze lands on Silas for a heartbeat—reminders passing wordlessly between them of cruel nights and hospital lights, of blood on wrists and hands shaken but never broken. Her scars tingle with the memory of old pain—the hot bite of a blade on her wrist once, a night of glass and smoke where Silas bled defending her, those moments in the wreckage when terror felt like drowning but love pulled them to air.

She remembers running before dawn with Silas, steps matched in synchronicity, the world chasing them but never quite catching up. Their bond was not born of easy days, but of surviving together when hope seemed like a fairy tale spun for fools. Now, she draws upon that same, stubborn resolve.

Her history is not spoken—no need. The weightiness in her tone is enough. In the past, she learned that wounds heal crooked, but the strength that follows is the kind that does not snap. It steadies hands, makes words ring like a bell in a place meant for secrets and shadows.

"You know what keeps us fighting?" she adds, her voice gentle but firm. "We remember why we started. Who we swore to protect. Let that shape us now. Let's find the real enemy—and do it as one."

A beat lingers. Seraphina nods. Elara's eyes shine with agreement, muting the tremble in Orion's hands. Lucien's jaw unclenches, a corner of his mouth twitching in reluctant respect. Mariel slides her pad aside, exchanging a look with Lila, both women's postures uncoiling, heads rising.

"They can try to break us," Darius murmurs, voice gravel-scraped but carrying the note Hana planted.

"But they won't," Seraphina adds, her defiance blooming in the gloom, "because the oath meant something, and it still does."

Shoulders relax by degrees. The weight of suspicion dissipates—not gone, but lightened, replaced by the smallest glimmer of trust rekindled. The Brotherhood's circle, though battered by doubt, realigns.

The final silence is not empty this time, but electric—a hush shot through with hope as each person's gaze drifts, inevitably, toward Hana, that flicker of light steadier than any doubt.

The underground war room pulses with a hush, charged with the tense breath of people who no longer quite trust the dark. Fiber optic stars shimmer in the domed ceiling, cold points of light spattered above the obsidian circle of the meeting table, casting faint constellations across grave faces. The brothers and their partners cluster close, shoulders brushing, but the room is tight with the sense of distances being measured anew. Screens blink with data—maps, personnel logs, security feeds—casting shifting lines across skin and steel. The air carries a subtle tang of static and cold stone, underscored by the faint, midnight musk of leather and something anxious and metallic beneath.

Caius leans over the table, skimming readouts that flicker in soft blue. The world he built should be unassailable; it's never bled like this before. His knuckles flex, betraying the riot beneath the calm. He glances at Seraphina, who stands just beside him, her steady presence a respite—her pulse visible at her throat, eyes darting from screen to face, searching for cracks.

Silas stands at the head, his voice low as he points to scrolling text on a security log. "We'll update all lockdown protocols—nightly encryption, silent alarms routed straight to our personal devices. I want hidden surveillance on every entry and exit, every handoff." Shadows pool beneath his eyes in the false starlight. "Access to outside communications goes through two encrypted channels, no exceptions. If any anomaly triggers, our defense funds divert instantly to secondary accounts under false shell names. No one, not even us, should feel safe with a single password."

Lucien's finger taps at digital event tags on a map, his tone precise. "We'll need selective monitoring by cohort. Every trace of access leaves a ghost. Mariel, we'll rely on your algorithms—scan for repeated anomalies, log every unusual bounce."

Mariel nods, already scribbling in a worn leather notebook. "I'll set up pattern detection. Behavior-based flags and AI cross-reference—anything strange will light up the board." Her words are clipped, but a note of determination edges them as her eyes meet Lucien's.

Darius wheels the floating interface to Lila, his voice gentler than before—a balm. "Lila and I will cross-check the background of everyone who's had physical or virtual access to restricted floors, all shifts. Staff, visitors, third-party contractors—no more blind spots."

Lila's lips tighten with resolve as she studies the transparent personnel sheet. "If we miss anything, it won't be for lack of looking. We'll run psychological profiling for stress markers—exhaustion, irritation, guilt. Maybe the traitor leaves a fingerprint in their behavior."

Orion, jaw set and eyes smoldering, breaks his silence. "And if we have to bait them, Elara and I can handle that. Trial runs—staged leaks, restricted data. We watch for who blinks, who runs to hide."

Elara nods, her hand settling on Orion's arm, anchoring him. "We'll play this carefully. No accusations, just patterns. Whoever's hiding has slipped up, and they will again."

Caius's gaze sweeps the circle, the weight of command visible in the set of his scarred jaw. "We layer the traps: dead drops with false information, silent trackers on every device. No one acts alone; two signatures, always. Seraphina will oversee the vulnerability audits—if the traitor's desperate, that's when they'll move."

Seraphina almost smiles, fierce and unyielding. "We won't give our enemy the chance to turn us against one another. They expect paranoia—let's give them precision."

Bare fingers trail the edge of polished wood. Trust, once their strongest weapon, is now as fragile as spun glass. Still, they gather—resentful, aching, but bound together.

"We can't let fear tear through what's left." Darius's voice is quiet, born of hours in the hospital midnight. "Unity kept us alive when the world wanted us to fall."

A beat of silence, heavier than the stone that cocooned them underground.

Lucien steps to the vault door, scanning the biometric lock until steel slides shut with a hush. "No more secrets between us—except the ones that protect us all. We move as one, or we don't move at all."

Eyes flicker from shadow to shadow, contact held just long enough to thread a line of trust, tentative but gleaming. Even here, where power was always currency, it's love—raw, desperate, frightened love—that keeps the circle unbroken for one last night.

Above the fiber optic stars, the constellations hold their places. Below, the Brotherhood—changed now, unsure—prepares, silent and watchful, unwilling to let the darkness win.

Council of Shadows

A muted chime pulses as Caius presses his fingertip to the scanner, the heavy biometric door sighing open on ancient hinges. He moves into the subterranean council chamber—deep beneath the city's skin, beneath noise, daylight, and ordinary laws. Amber sconces gutter on dark granite walls, throwing nervous shadows over the constellation-etched table at the room's center. Here, power is carved from darkness. In this place, secrets hang like condensation invisible in the cooled air, and the only sound for a moment is the soft click of his measured footsteps on polished stone. He pauses, letting his gaze sweep over granite so cold and smooth that his own reflection wavers near the surface—a king in a world built on whispers.

Lucien enters, the soft hiss of his suit jacket barely audible. He stands in the doorway, sharp-eyed and composed, his presence an icicle glinting in the half-light. His gaze finds Darius's cautious nod across the chamber before he moves with unhurried confidence to a high-backed leather chair, the constellation crest reflected in the deep black of his sleeve. He sits, hands folded, every inch the strategist holding chaos at bay beneath a pressed collar.

Darius's arrival is the merest hush—a breath of movement. Lila is at his side, her hand clutching his arm just above the wrist, knuckles pale. Darius's nod to Silas is all tension and brittle truce, and Lila's eyes flick instinctively across the room, reading currents, seeking reassurance. Silas lingers back near the velvet-draped wall, blue eyes narrowed, suspicion drawn tight along his jawline.

The chamber swallows the sound as Orion pushes through the door, Elara just behind. He stops, the air around him charged, tension etched in every taut sinew from clamped jaw to clenched fists. Elara's presence is a whisper of calm—she moves closer, her fingers brushing his back, steadying, tempering the storm in his bones. Their entrance hushes the low murmur of preparations; each face turns as if waiting for a signal, a spark, an eruption.

Silas's gloved hand closes the doors. The final barrier. He scans the faces ringing the table: Hana has already found her seat, calm on the surface, but her eyes betray a deep, rippling unease.

Caius stands at the head, his figure dark against the constellation motif in the ceiling above. "Enough. We begin." His voice is iron wrapped in restraint, reverberating around the granite that has heard a hundred secrets and a thousand lies. "Betrayal has been carried in on the same boots that once guarded this room. We sit here because every bond is at risk. There's nothing more urgent than absolute honesty. If you can't offer it, speak now."

No one does.

Lucien's voice cuts the silence, subtle as a stiletto. "Security isn't breached by ghosts. Someone within these walls provided help. Those attacks—too precise, too timed." His eyes, glinting, hold each of them in turn—Darius, Silas, Orion. Mariel's breath stirs sharply; she does not look away.

Darius leans forward, crafting each word as if it could wound or save. "Who last accessed the encrypted files? Not speculation—proof." The table absorbs the weight of his stare. Silas says nothing, lips flattened, jaw locked, the silence heavy as accusation itself.

Orion's patience snaps, his voice rough as gravel scraping beneath the coffin lid. "Is everyone here telling the truth? Or have we been playing defender while someone played us for fools?" He points—a quick, jarring movement—at the table, at fate itself. "I want answers. Tonight." Elara's hand finds his forearm. Her touch is meadow-soft, a silent plea. He feels the edge, returning from it by degrees.

Caius's slap of fist on wood wrenches every eye. His pain is thunder in the bones of the room. "Enough." The tremor flows out from the table's heart, quelling dissent. "We will not end as some cautionary tale. We built a world in the absence of daylight. But the shadows we command harbor knives for our backs. We don't leave here clinging to suspicion—every member, every partner must cooperate. Or we will fall, one by one."

They hang there on the edge, suspended while the spiral of their own secrecy closes around them. The silent consensus takes root—wordless but absolute. There is no path left but the hunt for the traitor, and in this moment, trust is both the rarest coin and the most dangerous weapon.

Their secret brotherhood was designed for control, for an empire built unseen—yet every hidden fortress is only a shell, every shadow a possible gallows. The stakes swell beneath the stone: not just fortunes and territories, but the lives they have bound together, the love born from fire and steel. If the hidden heart of their power is breached, everything ends—not with a storm, but rot from within.

Caius feels the ache of history pressing in—the loyalty demanded, the burdens carried, the knowledge that his strengths have become both shield and prison. Night after night, he wonders if all he built is only shards balanced on regret and vigilance. He wears a mask of control, steady as granite, but behind it, the fault lines run deep. He'll not show the fissures. Not tonight.

So they remain, seven pairs of wary eyes, caged together in the dim light, each breath a testament to a trust already battered. Above, the painted stars watch—unblinking, indifferent, warning of constellations that can shatter as easily as glass.

The glow of Lucien's tablet slices the darkness, its pale blue graph branching out across the surface of the council table, mirrored in the polished obsidian beneath. Small pinpricks of amber reflect on tense faces. His fingertip glides along the digital network map, the lines trembling as if the Brotherhood's entire foundation is perilously thin.

"The breaches don't come from outside," Lucien says quietly, each word clipped and deliberate. "We will surveil every message, every keystroke, every sensor in our properties starting now." The network laces itself spider-like across the screen—entry points, encrypted protocols, dead ends that aren't as dead as they should be.

Mariel leans in, the steady rhythm of her breath brushing Lucien's sleeve. Her gaze, sharp beneath the constellation tattoo on her forearm, lifts to meet his. There's a language in their silence as she double-taps a node on the map, and Lucien hands her the surveillance keys. "You'll lead with me." He keeps his voice flat, but a twitch of his jaw betrays the memory of sabotage haunting his mind. Not again. Not her. Not if he can stop it.

Across the table, Lila breaks the hush. Her voice is low, unwavering. "If the traitor's among us, he'll slip eventually." She glances at Darius, who nods—silent, solid as old stone. Lila's fingers move on her datapad, creating honeytrap vulnerabilities, cracks just wide enough to tempt the guilty. Data leaks poised, candies for a spy to snatch. Darius sketches flowcharts beside her, their heads near, hands overlapping as plans take shape. Each tap, each shuffle of paper between them, is a wordless, stubborn dance—daring betrayal away from their doorstep.

Silas sits unmoving in the half-light, a quiet anchor with a hawkish stare fixed on his own reflection in the granite. When he speaks at last, it slices the room clean. "Keep your secrets cleaner than your hands. Leak nothing." His gaze burns into their ranks, lingering on the folders the others possess. "No more whispers outside this circle. Our most delicate contacts—their lives are forfeit if even a shadow falls in the wrong place." Beneath his words, a rare strain trembles—defensive, almost desperate. Hana's hand finds his, a fleeting squeeze hidden under the table. All she offers is her presence, grounding him.

Caius stands, not at the head so much as between every fracture. He watches the dossier folders pass down the circle, the Brotherhood's future reduced to rustling envelopes and inked assignment lists—Caius and Seraphina: physical audits and personnel sweeps; Lucien and Mariel: digital tracking, cyber forensics; Darius and Lila: backgrounds, histories resurrected for fresh scrutiny; Silas and Hana: covert observation, reading trust in smiles and stares. Each couple receives sealed, crimson-marked files. The gesture, once routine, now feels like a challenge, a weighing of alliances. The names on the covers aren't just tasks—they're declarations of trust and, for some, wagers of faith.

Seraphina brushes past Lucien as she accepts her file, a bright flame against his shadowed resolve. He doesn't meet her eyes. Not now, with so much to lose. At the opposite end, Orion grinds his teeth, knuckles white, and Elara murmurs to him—soft, steady, always the anchor, never the storm.

Lucien can feel the currents shifting, sharp as glass on bare skin. The air in the chamber shimmers with friction—the scrape of suspicion, the unspoken rivalries, the memory of old failures. Eyes flit, wrists flex, lips part but say nothing. Trust, here, is currency weighed by hesitation and staked on secrets never fully spent. Even Mariel, his confidante, sits stiff beside him, her knee angled away just slightly—a barricade or a shield. All of them form up as pairs, but the unity is surface-deep. Underneath, the memory of betrayal pools like oil on water.

He recalls the laboratory, the night Mariel's work was corrupted—how she'd hidden her wounded pride behind a façade of logic, how rage had simmered in him as he combed through lines of code, finding only emptiness where there should be security. Every step since, every code and protocol, has become a wall he leans on now, refusing to let the past crack this shell. He trusts no one but her—almost not even her, if he's honest in the bruised recesses of his mind.

Caius's voice slices through the tension. "This investigation does not exist beyond this room. Fail, and the Brotherhood dies here." His words ignite a silent agreement—not of hope, but of necessity.

As the session ends, dossiers clutched to chests, they rise one by one. Determination carves their features as each couple drifts into the corridors beyond, the lights behind them flickering and dimming, and the thick, velvet darkness swallowing doubt and alliance alike.

Lucien's fingers grip the edge of his datapad as faint blue light reflects off its glass, glinting in the half-dark of the chamber. He leans toward Mariel, his voice pitched just low enough to slip beneath the radar of suspicious ears. Footsteps echo off the granite walls, a subtle counter-rhythm to words weighted by implication.

"They're covering their tracks too well," he murmurs, jaw tight. "Attendance records for the guard rotation—two entries are missing. Intentional or oversight?" His eyes flick to Darius across the table, then back to Mariel. Anxiety stirs beneath his polished control.

Mariel's hand, steady and elegant, rests on the constellation-tattooed notebook in her lap. Her brow furrows, lips barely parted as she scans the table, senses picking up the restless energy, the pulse of a gathering storm. She meets his gaze—a silent question, asking if he trusts her more than the weight of invisible threats pressing in on all sides.

A hush grows between the seats, thick as fog. Darius, his voice spent to a whisper, leans into Lila's ear. "Anyone seen Orion leave the perimeter logs unsigned again?" Suspicion traces thin fissures along his careful mask, his eyes narrowly trained on the gaps in movement records. Lila's grip tightens on his wrist—one finger tracing over a pulse that leaps in time with uncertainty. She darts a glance at Orion, who sits rigid, unreadable behind a veil of shadow, his silhouette braced somewhere between flight and attack.

Orion's posture stiffens. The tension in his neck jumps, as if some unseen wire pulled tight inside his skin. Elara, never far, brushes his knuckles under the obsidian light. He catches her touch but shakes his head, gaze snapping back to the distorted reflection of the chamber in the thick glass wall. Outside, nothing stirs, but inside, trust crackles and pops—a slow electrical burn.

Seraphina moves quickly, her footfalls quiet but purposeful, intercepting Silas at the threshold as the meeting breaks for a moment. Her eyes are dark, urgent. She corners him with her question—words sharp, honed on worry and anger.

"Silas, you knew about the breach two days ago. Why wait till now to say anything?" Her voice cuts, the syllables catching on years of learned caution.

Silas's lips pull into a brittle line. "I don't disclose half-baked evidence. We need hard proof, not more chaos. You know that." His words are crisp, but pride glimmers behind the coolness, deeper currents rippling beneath the surface.

Seraphina's jaw clenches. "Your silence gives them time. The longer you wait, the more danger we're in. Are you shielding someone?" The accusation sizzles in the air.

Silas turns away, features hardening under the fluorescent glare gathering along his sharp cheekbones. "You're looking for a scapegoat, not a solution." His voice is low but brittle, the edge of a blade dulled by exhaustion. Hana, silent in the hallway, sees the tremor in Silas's hands, the way he clasps them behind his back to still their shaking.

Orion—unable to bear the tightening coil—withdraws into a dim alcove where the air is colder, thinner. His outline seems blurred by fractured light, arms folded protectively across his chest. He watches through the glass as the others pull apart, eyes raw with disappointment. Elara steps in quietly, her voice almost lost in the hum of hidden machinery.

"Orion." Her tone is soft—a drop of water striking stone. He doesn't turn, just shakes his head once, lips pressed to a rigid line. She stays near, not touching, but lending her steadiness to his shadow. He never lets himself unravel where others can see.

Inside the chamber, Lucien's thoughts churn. Every missing answer, every unsaid word allows suspicion to bloom. Patterns unfurl in his mind: attendance anomalies, shift swaps, hastily erased digital traces. He wants—needs—order, auditable certainty. Yet paranoia breeds secrets, drives distance between him and Mariel, the only person he trusts to see his fears naked. Even now, their hands graze but don't grasp. He longs for her reassurance yet cannot surrender his vigilance, caught between needing her closeness and fearing the cost of misplaced faith.

Caius stands, clearing his throat, his presence looming over the scattered council. His fist raps the constellation-emblazoned table, the sound echoing through the cavernous stone.

"Enough. Trust has become our most dangerous weapon—and our greatest risk. Every eye is watching. Every word may be twisted. Anyone hiding truth, anyone gambling with our future, must understand: next time, we unleash consequences none of you have faced before. We survive by vigilance. Nothing less."

The words ring out, final and cold. No one argues.

One by one, the Brotherhood spills into the silent corridors, burdened by more than coded dossiers and encrypted tablets. Lucien lingers in the gloom, watching the sweep of Mariel's hair as she turns away, the scent of her lingering—a mix of neroli and tension. Sound filters out: the low hiss of the air systems, the click of dress shoes on stone, the slow, mechanical hum of the chamber door drawing shut, cutting them off from the city above. Inside the darkness, fear gnaws at resolve, suspicion devours comfort, and the ancient, deadly question loops in every mind—can loyalty survive the fractures in the foundation, or is something vital lost the moment you lock the chamber door?

The Ultimatum

Night pools along the black marble floors of the Brotherhood's sanctum, every surface catching the low, golden glint of recessed lights. A hush lingers thick as velvet in the corridors that connect power to secrecy, broken only by the soft pads of Hana's shoes. She stands at the threshold, one foot inside the circle of honeyed light beneath a security panel, her phone alive in her palm—a pale rectangle of assurance. Air whispers with the aftertaste of council debates, heavy with the threat of betrayal and the sweet, sharp tang of adrenaline that always hangs in these halls.

A sudden bloom of pressure, a displacement of air—three figures unravel from the darkness. No footfalls. The service door gapes behind them, wide as a wound. The tactical gear they wear drinks the light, giving back nothing. Hana lifts her head, a question half-formed on her lips. Black-gloved hands clamp across her arms. A zip of panic twists her face. She's wrenched sideways, her phone tumbling, her gasp swallowed before it can become a scream. The jagged imprint of her alarm badge blinks crimson as she's carried, silent, through the service gap now swallowing all evidence of innocence.

In the adjoining lounge, laughter flickers weakly between tired voices—Caius flattening his hands on a table edge, Lucien sketching strategies in the air, Orion cracking his knuckles like rolling thunder. Lila straightens the lapel of Darius's jacket, her touch a silent reminder of love's shield. The air hums with anticipation, the sense that something unresolved tugs beneath their carefully ordered world.

A shrill alarm hacks through the calm, trilling from somewhere close and yet impossibly far. Silas's spine snaps straight. His face drains to winter. The others freeze—a tableau carved from shock.

He's out the door before anyone else moves, each stride echoing dread. The hallway stares back at him, mercilessly untouched, except for the objects lying there: Hana's phone, its screen spider-webbed, an unblinking red signal pulsating; and a black card, thick and lacquered, a stylized silver serpent coiling with quiet menace. The scent of sweat and ozone still lingers as if violence has a taste.

Silas drops to his knees. His hand tightens around the phone until his knuckles blanch. For a moment, he is nothing but a trembling exhale, shoulders caving as the past—the old terror of losing everything—rips through him anew.

Darius's footsteps thunder up behind him. He stops short, eyes wide. "Silas—God. What happened? Where is she?" His hands hover, not daring to touch, afraid that the smallest pressure will shatter the man in front of him. Orion barrels past, unleashing a wild, bestial snarl, his fist slamming into the nearest wall. Plaster powder snows down, sharp and bitter in the air.

Lila presses both hands to her lips, her body folding inward. Her voice is lost, leaking only through wide, wet eyes.

"Lock every exit. No one leaves. No one gets in," Caius spits through the comm, his voice knife-blade sharp. "Find out how they got past us—now!"

Seraphina stalks behind him, her voice daubed with panic, edges softening and breaking. "How did they do it? We checked every protocol twice—this place is supposed to be a fortress!"

Lucien angles his head toward Mariel, eyes like glass. "There must have been a blind spot, something—someone—inside," he mutters low. Mariel's mind races, lips moving as she tallies threats, parsing every stolen second for clues.

"Elara." Silas's voice is ragged, small, pleading for her calm. Her hand drapes over his shoulder. "We'll get her back, Silas. They want something. That keeps her alive." Her reassurance trembles, words quaking like leaves in a storm.

Caius's orders splinter the room. "No mistakes. Sweep every feed. Expect a message—this is a declaration, not a random attack. They want us off-balance."

A current of dread binds the group. The circle closes, bodies drawing near, united by fear, suspicion flickering in every glance. Only minutes ago, this stronghold gleamed, prideful, its every alarm and scanner a promise: no one penetrates the Brotherhood. Now, their illusion has shattered. The sanctuary that stood as a monument to power—cameras in every corner, locks keyed to blood and bone—lies broken. There's a cruel elegance in the breach. Centuries of secret war pulse through the veins of the world, one hidden society always shadowing another, each new generation thinking themselves untouchable until shadows drag their loved ones away.

Inside Silas, numbness gives way to a turbulent sea of shame. His life has been an exercise in control—every secret, every plan a shield. What good is vigilance now, when the one he loves most is stolen from behind those perfect layers? His mind claws for answers, rewriting every moment between them: Did he see it coming? Did he miss a plea for comfort? He digs his nails into the phone, steel in his jaw. If secrecy built these walls, what if that same secrecy razed them? He swears he'll raze the world to bring her back. This pain, raw and pure, carves him open—leader, lover, shadow. There is nothing left to lose.

Caius stands amid them, his jaw granite, anger folding with helplessness. Around him, the Brotherhood is no longer indivisible—cracked, exposed, suddenly so mortal.

Silas's voice is a whisper, hoarse and trembling: "I'll bring her home. Or die trying." The vow slices through the hush, and in its wake, consequence tastes bitter—like iron, like ash—in every mouth.

The Brotherhood's secure command center hums with latent menace—deep in the sub-basement, far below the city's surface claws and neon provocations. The air tastes metallic, the polished granite beneath their feet cold and absolute, shadows sliding over the walls where amber light tries—and fails—to soften the room's brutal edges. Caius leads the way, his silhouette framed by the wall of screens blinking with the fractured constellation of their security systems. He's flanked by Silas, drawn and shaking, and Lucien, face carved in iron. The others spill in after, their steps echoing—Orion's haunted energy, Darius's clenched resolve, Mariel's flashing eyes already scanning for cracks in the fortress, Lila barely holding herself upright, Seraphina's arms folded hard across her chest, Elara a silent, steady anchor.

Caius's voice, flint meeting steel, pierces the silence. "Activate the comm. Now. Direct channel." The technician's hands tremble against the keys. Caius can't let his own fingers betray the tremor coiled through his veins—he must appear unbreakable, even as the old fear gnaws at him from the inside, the fear that he has failed them, again.

The main monitor flares to life. The rival leader's face floods the room: half in shadow, the jagged scar gleaming on his jaw, eyes sharp as razors. He sits with the composure of a chess master—untouchable, clinical, aware that every second tilts the world more in his favor. A cold click; he presses a key. Another feed blooms next to him: Hana, hands bound behind her, seated in a steel chair in a cell stripped bare as bone. Stark light slants across her face, making her appear both fragile and dangerously alive.

The leader's voice is smooth, with a chill that seeps into the marrow. "Surrender. Full transfer of operational control, all assets, by midnight. Or, Hana dies." No thunder, no bravado, just the matter-of-fact tone of someone well accustomed to drawing lines in blood.

Silas lurches forward, fists balled at his sides. Lucien draws in a careful breath, eyes flickering over the data trailing at the screen's margins.

A dialogue erupts, compressed and lethal as lightning.

"You think we'll kneel for you?" Caius's growl carries the weight of his broken childhood and every oath he's ever sworn.

"I think, tonight, you'll decide what you love most: power, or her." The leader's gaze flicks to Hana. "This isn't chess, Caius. It's checkmate. There are no moves left."

"Prove she's alive." Caius spits the words.

In the feed, Hana raises her head, eyes burning. She blinks twice—an old signal for distress. Silas's lips part in a silent prayer. Darius's knuckles go white against polished granite.

Caius pushes harder. "More time."

"No." The leader's voice slices—final, pitiless. "You may say goodbye. Once. Then accept the cost." The screen pulses red: one hour.

As the leader turns away, Silas's voice fractures, ragged, desperate. "Let her go. Your war isn't with her; it's with us. I'll give you anything—take me instead. Please."

The rival's eyes narrow. "Every empire has its sacrifices. Choose quickly. You have sixty minutes. Anything less, and her blood is on your hands."

"My hands are clean!" Silas bursts out, but the screen has already cut to static.

Lucien steps in, voice tight but measured. "Where is she? This—" His fingers dart over the encrypted feed—"doesn't look like any facility we've mapped. You're playing us."

No answer. Only the leader's dry, unblinking silence. "It's simple. Surrender, or lose her. You have nothing left to negotiate." The feed crackles, the cell dissolves in pixelated distortion.

In the corner, Mariel scribbles notes, eyes glued to every flicker—room angles, light, the way Hana's shadow moves—searching for a trace to chase. Lila's shoulders hunch as tears shiver down her cheeks, each drop hitting her palm a small, bitter defeat. Darius's jaw works—they've survived betrayals before, but this is the kind of cruelty that seeps into your bones and reshapes you. Orion stalks the edge of the group, feet grinding against cold stone, unable to stand still—Elara's touch steadies his shoulder, her thumb tracing circles that promise, not yet, not yet.

Caius watches all of them—the fractures beneath their armor, the tiny betrayals of breath and posture. He has to keep them tethered; if he unravels, the whole constellation falls apart. His mind runs inventory: options, dangers, their network bleeding weakness under the pressure. He aches for a plan that can be both ruthless and merciful, but the world won't let him have both. Not tonight.

The rival leader's image blinks once more, final as a dirge. "One hour. Make your choice."

The connection severs. Static floods the room—a tinnitus whine, unmooring even the strongest. The group stands together, and yet every one of them is miles away, alone with the cost.

Caius lowers his head, breath held hostage in his chest, hands clenched so tightly he can feel the old scar tug along his knuckles. He forces his voice steady, each word chiseled in stone. "Sixty minutes. That's all we've got. Every decision counts—get ready."

The seconds drip away, and in the air—sharper than blood, heavier than iron—lurks the truth: not all of them will make it out whole.

Candlelight flickers across the sanctuary's curved stone walls, casting shifting constellations upon velvet and marble. Shadows coil in silent recesses, softening the burnished gold of the Brotherhood's sigil overhead. The air stirs with the scent of warm beeswax and old books—sanctuary, but not safety. Seraphina's body sinks into the embrace of a plum velvet chair set alone beneath one arched window. Her breath comes shallow, fingertips pressing the armrests taut, anchoring herself before a tide she can't command.

Near her hip, the silk of her dress feels slick with sweat. Her pulse thrums in her temple, matching the insistent tick of a hidden clock. Hana's face hovers before her—bright, then pale as a ghost. In her mind, choices scatter like glass: accept the rival's brutal bargain, or defy them and risk Hana's life crumbling between their fingers. The empire, she thinks. The Brotherhood. Is there a future where love isn't the prelude to ruin?

Her scars itch beneath the silk sleeve—old, puckered reminders that bravery is not a guarantee. She remembers running once, through a night like this, past warning bells and wet alleyways, shouts on the air. She'd paid with blood and bone for protection and walked away still unfinished, more afraid of losing those she loved than of her own wounds. Some losses never really heal; they burrow into your heartbeat, waiting for moments like this.

Across the room, Lucien and Mariel stand cocooned in the sanctuary's alcove—her voice low, his reply brittle. Their silhouettes are sheared sharp by candlelight, tension snapping in the narrow space between them.

"We can't allow ourselves to be backed into a corner like this—surrender now, and we're not just defeated, we're done. They'll gut us in the open, one by one," Lucien says, crisp and cold.

"And if we don't?" Mariel's arms wrap around herself, shoulders hunched. "Hana dies, and the rest of us... will you ever forgive yourself for that?"

Lucien's face hardens. His gaze flickers to the stone floor, jaw flexing as if words grind between his teeth. "An empire isn't built for mercy. We don't trade everything for one life. If we do, none of us are safe."

A silence stretches. Mariel's fingers twist the edge of her sleeve, voice wavering. "So we sacrifice her for survival?"

A quiet scoff, bitter at the edges. "Rationality protects more than hope."

Light from a dozen candles trembles over Darius as he paces before a sprawling map speared with colored pins. He mutters half to Lila, half to the ghosts only he hears. "If we surrender now, we feed them. Every future enemy will know—take one, and the rest fall."

Lila steps into his path. Her voice quivers, brave if not steady. "Darius. This isn't a faceless casualty. It's Hana. If you were the one gone—would you want us to weigh you like an asset?"

He halts, lips twisting as guilt flares beneath his eyes. "It's not the same."

"Isn't it? How many times did you ask that question in the hospital, when the whispers got too close, when people you cared about fell anyway?" she asks. "There's always a 'greater good.' But what if it's just fear, dressed as reason?"

Darius reaches for her hand, voice stripped raw. "I can't keep losing. I can't."

Across the sanctuary, Orion sits hunched on a leather bench, elbows braced on knees as he scrolls, thumb trembling, through old photos—Nova laughing at dusk, storms for eyes. Rain ghosts the windows. Lightning, somewhere distant. Silas leans against a stone column, shoulders drawn too tight, breath shuddering as his grip whitens his knuckles. Shadows climb his cheeks as memories drag him under—a hundred moments where he was too slow, not enough, lives slipping through his grasp.

Elara stands by, still as stone and soft as dusk, her eyes fixed on Orion, feeling the storm beneath his skin as if it thunders through her own.

Seraphina watches them, mind spiraling out—what if we let Hana die? What if we all fall? She imagines the empire hollow and cold, their names remembered not as legends, but as cautionary tales in forgotten rooms. If they surrender, do they survive as ghosts of themselves? If they risk it all, who will be left to gather the ashes?

A thousand futures bloom, each with its own taste of loss.

She closes her eyes, inhaling candlewax, dust, the metallic scent of fear. Her scars prickle, quiet reminders of pain and love entwined—the only certainty she's ever known is that she cannot protect everyone, no matter how fierce her heart. Maybe love is a battle where both victory and defeat leave wounds. Still, she clings to hope, fragile as the flame licking the wick near her hand.

Caius's voice cuts through the hush, rough as stone broken by tide. He gathers them, one by one, into the sanctuary's heart. Every face flickers with exhaustion and dread—choices carving new scars across all of them—as his shadow stretches long against the candlelit walls, and he begins to outline what comes next.

Night Before Fate

The city glows beneath black glass, sharp as a memory, the skyline painted in jeweled flecks against Caius's penthouse windows. The air carries the faintest tang of ozone—rain threatening at the edges, the metallic tang of old storms and distant sirens drifting from far below. The study is a fortress of shadows: walls lined in deep mahogany, a desk scarred yet gleaming, the rich perfume of dark leather mingling with a smoky thread of cognac in the air. Seraphina stands near the window, her reflection double-paned—a woman carved out of darkness and light, her scar visible in the low luminescence.

Caius watches her, his hands pressed flat on the desk. His knuckles are pale, betraying the effort it takes not to reach for her immediately. Outside, the city seems endless, but intimacy—real and dangerous—fills the space with a heat no fire could match.

He finds his voice first, the words earned rather than given. "Do you remember that night, Sera? When the Brotherhood nearly fell?" His tone holds an edge honed over years of command yet softened, for once, by blunt honesty. "You stood between me and a bullet that belonged to someone else. If I close my eyes, I can taste the gunpowder—hear that window shatter again."

A silence falls, and in it, every shadow seems to draw closer. Seraphina's stance shifts; her arms fold across her chest, lips pressing into a defiant line, but her eyes don't look away. "I wasn't thinking. Not really. Just... there was no world I wanted to walk through where you weren't standing next to me." The cityscape gleams in her eyes, but her gaze is unflinching. "They wanted you scared. Alone. And I—I couldn't let them win."

Caius breathes in, the memory tightening in his chest—years of solitude cracking along old fault lines. That night, chaos pressed in from every angle. Betrayal erupted from within council chambers, gunmen revealed as brothers, the taste of smoke slick against his tongue. He'd always trusted his own resilience, but he hadn't understood the cost of love until he saw Seraphina drop to shield him, blood welling at the sleeve of her blouse—a single, defiant stroke of crimson against the black.

He recalls the way power seemed to slip through his fingers as two empires collided, how the very notion of control turned to glass. Yet the moment she fell, something inside him snapped—old armor shed, a new vow forged between the rush of footsteps and the sting of antiseptic. Trust, real trust, wasn't built from alliances or threats. It was her, battered but unbroken, choosing him even as ruin spread in every direction.

For a while, the only sound is the city rumbling below, the tick of an unseen clock.

"I never thanked you," Caius says softly, moving closer. His fingers find the scar on her arm. "That night... you saw through every lie I built to keep the world at arm's length. I thought I was the one protecting you. Hell, maybe I tried too hard." His throat works, unsteady.

"But you broke me open, Seraphina. I've never let anyone stand so close and stay."

Seraphina's laugh is small, strangled—half sob, half relief. She unfolds, stepping into his space. "You don't have to thank me. You never have to." She slides her hand up the back of his neck, warm and real, grounding him. "But if tonight really is the calm before it all breaks again, I want you to know... I would do it every time. For you."

Beneath the glass and steel, the city doesn't stop. Somewhere, beneath their feet, a siren wails. Inside the study, though, time stills—two people daring to name the cost of survival.

On the balcony of Lucien's suite, dusk falls heavy, cool air edged with the scent of wet stone and lavender. Mariel sits curled into a teak chair, fingers worrying at the constellation inked on her arm, the city lights twinkling like distant promises. Lucien leans against the railing, tie loosened, watching her with eyes that betray centuries of worry.

"I haven't been sleeping," Mariel admits, her voice low. "Your past—it's a shadow I can't see around. Sometimes I wonder, if all this falls apart, will you let me in before you walk away, or just leave me in the dark?"

Quiet seeps between them.

Lucien kneels beside her, his careful composure splintering. "If I drift too far into the dark, pull me back. I can't promise I'll never falter, but I swear you'll never face it alone." He threads his fingers through hers, the warmth of his skin a silent pledge.

Elsewhere, in a hospital apartment washed in amber lamplight, Darius perches at the mattress edge. Across from him, Lila—hair tucked behind one ear, worry lines softening as she meets his gaze.

"When they came for the hospital, for everything I built, you stayed," Darius says, his voice rough. "Your faith didn't just heal patients. It healed me."

Lila smiles, resilient, the echo of loss and sabotage lingering unspoken. "Every test we faced, you held me steady. That's how I know—whatever comes next, we cross together."

Among rows of ancient books, Orion sprawls in a leather chair, storm-blue eyes shadowed, half-lost in memory. Elara sits opposite, feet curled beneath her, candlelight gilding the curve of her smile.

"Nova almost died because I was reckless," Orion mutters, his head bowed. "If you hadn't—" His words choke off.

Elara reaches, steady as a heartbeat. "You brought me hope when you had none left. Some storms need two anchors. I'm not going anywhere."

In a fractured alcove, moonlight trickles over glass shards and bare concrete. Silas sits tense, hands trembling until Hana covers them, gentle as dawn breaking the longest night.

"I dragged you into danger you never deserved," his confession is raw.

Hana's answer is simple, unwavering. "You gave me a choice. I chose you. That's as brave as anything I've done."

Across the city, as the minutes slip toward fate, arms lock—embraces silent and shaping—love steeling itself beneath the brittle hush of before.

Night glides in thick and heavy through the penthouse windows, sinking into the glass and iron bones of Caius's domain. Shadows slice through the secure conference room, where amber LEDs cast reflections across sheets of digital blueprints and scrolling data on cold, humming screens. The city below thrums, a distant heart—but here, suspense is syrup-thick, clinging even in breath.

Caius holds the room's gravity. His posture is unyielding, but small betrayals give him away—a hand flexing along the ebony table edge, the muscle in his jaw twitching. Against the backdrop of scrolling threat reports, he commands focus without raising his voice. Around him, the Brotherhood and their partners—Seraphina, Lucien, Mariel, Darius, Lila, Orion, Elara, Silas, and Hana—form a loose constellation, each face up-lit with flickers of hope and dread. Their reflections stain the glossy table like ghosts.

"Gala intel's confirmed," Caius murmurs, scanning the labyrinthine security diagram. "Four entrances, two disguised service elevators, one emergency crawlspace here—" His finger taps. The echo rings sharp. "Interception's their game. Ours is getting in and out with everyone breathing."

Lucien's tone cuts sideways, measured as always: "I can have the back channels rerouted. If they're compromising ID badges, we scrub the signals—use biometrics only."

Orion leans close, tense as a thunderhead, scrolling another intercepted message onto the main monitor. "We go in loud, we're corpses. Go in too soft, we're ghosts. Give me the lock rotation code for the ballroom, and five minutes with the ventilation grid."

A thin note of tension slips into Mariel's voice. "The rival's trigger team can change positioning in twelve seconds. We're gambling on our fallback routes."

Darius, calm anchored in exhaustion, counters, "We won't leave anyone behind. Not this time."

On the periphery, Lila's hand finds Darius's under the table, squeezing against the hush of anxiety. Elara's gaze flicks between Orion's restless hands and the blue-glowing exits, cataloging risks, trust settling in the fold between them. The scent of coffee—sharp, medicinal, almost burning—cuts the recycled air, a reminder that focus must conquer fatigue.

Underneath the surface, waves of old memory roll through Caius. Once, he mistook unity for armor—made of glass, not steel. Scars pulse along his cheek and his soul, reminding him that power demands both distance and sacrifice. Now, the Brotherhood is less a shield than a fragile living thing, its veins running right through the woman at his side, through every risk written in the eyes that meet his. He wants to believe he isn't failing. He has to.

A soft mechanical whirr: Silas and Hana slide back from the main huddle, alcove shadows swallowing their movements. Silas cracks open a black steel case, velvet-wrapped inside with a sidearm—matte barrel marked by his initials. Hana draws forth her med kit and a blade, slim and pale as bone. They pass the objects between them, knuckles brushing, promises exchanged without a word—no hesitation, only the silent pact of those who love in a world perpetually ready to burn.

Orion and Elara mutter in soft, rapid fire; bright screens spill radiance over their skin. Orion toggles encrypted comms, lips tightening as connections flicker and resolve. Elara cross-references escape protocols—her finger trails each exit on the screen, her voice low as mist. She leans close, her warmth cutting the sterile, electric chill.

Dialogue shifts within the charged circle:

"This isn't just another job," Seraphina says, standing firm beneath Caius's steady look. "You're not alone at the eye of this. None of us are."

Caius allows his hand to fall over hers, pulse thrilling at the connection, his voice gritty. "You think I don't know that? I feel every one of you here. Especially when I'm supposed to stand apart." His thumb strokes the inside of her wrist. "Tomorrow—whatever comes, I'll find you. No chaos, no shadows. That's my vow."

Across the table, Mariel's words coil around Lucien's defenses: "You told me once that trust was risk, not certainty. I need you to risk with me tomorrow. Not just calculation. All of you."

Lucien draws her closer. "You're my anchor. No riddle, no past—just us. I won't leave you adrift. Not again."

A hush falls, collective breaths synchronizing, then slow splitting—each couple pulled into their own orbit. Darius wraps Lila in his arms, foreheads brushing. "We get through this, or not at all. You and I? Indivisible."

Lila leans into him, unblinking. "Strength isn't fighting alone—it's fighting for someone. That's us."

Elara's hand slides into Orion's. "No storm breaks us. You run, I hold the ground. You fly, I light the way."

Hana whispers to Silas, her voice a silk thread. "If it all falls, love is what we build back from. It's always been you."

The room folds in around Caius. He sees every fracture, every flash of hope, the fierce, stubborn refusal to abandon love even when night presses hard against the glass. These are not soldiers. They are the only world left that matters.

One by one, couples slip from the circle, footfalls muffled as they pass through corridors thick with darkness, hearts cinched tight around dread and devotion. The door closes behind the last, and silence drops—a pause, not an end. The night waits, holding its breath.

Beyond Caius's floor-to-ceiling windows, the city burns with midnight electricity—skyscrapers cut from glass and silver glimmer against a blue-black sky, the world holding its breath on the edge of tomorrow. Inside, the suite hums with a softer light: brushed gold sconces melt shadows into the walls, refracting warmth over the tray on the table—half-empty wine glasses, the last scarlet dribble reflecting memories and promises.

Seraphina is in his arms, her head resting in the hollow where his shoulder meets his heart. Her hair smells faintly of wild jasmine, a scent that lingers long after dusk. Caius's hand, rough with old scars, draws idle circles between her shoulder blades. When he breathes in, he tastes a cocktail of city rain, wool, and Seraphina's skin—a mingling that anchors him here, away from the clutter of strategy and war rooms. For this brief spell, the world outside can burn and the Brotherhood's fate can hang, trembling, above his head; inside, he is only a man who has spent most of his life learning how to survive, and far less learning how to love.

He kisses her, shedding the last vestiges of calculated control. There is no hesitation—just the fierce, aching press of lips that have tasted fear and adrenaline and, now, peace. Seraphina seizes the moment, fingers twining in his hair, pulling him into the present with a desperation that feels less like fear and more like hunger. Their bodies align naturally, as if the world were designed for this thumbprint of time: shared breaths, soft laughter, the unspooling of tension in a touch. The suite is silent except for the slide of fabric against skin, the hush of breath, the city's hum beyond glass.

"Don't let go," she whispers, her voice low and raw as tempest winds over distant water.

"Never." Caius answers with a rough certainty he cannot summon in a boardroom. His thumb traces the faded scar along his cheek—he remembers a warehouse, gunfire, the metallic reek of blood and burning flesh. Once, Seraphina had shielded him, thrown herself into danger with an impulse that had nothing to do with strategy and everything to do with trust. That memory flares behind his eyes now, colored by fear and gratitude. He cradles her closer, as if holding her body could ward off fate's teeth.

Light spills across the sheets, casting bronze shadows over Seraphina's chest. The scent of her hair grounds Caius in the here and now. She pulls back enough to search his face, her thumb pressing into the edge of his jaw, her eyes filled with stubborn hope and exhaustion.

"We've made it this far," she says, her voice just above the city's pulse. "If tomorrow tries to break us, we break it first."

"We do more than survive," he murmurs. "We endure."

"Promise me, Caius. No lies. No walls."

He smiles—not the cruel twist he wears for adversaries, or the thin-lipped mask for business partners, but something rare and open. "I promise." The words vibrate in his chest, terrifying in their sincerity.

Elsewhere, the city glows—Lucien shares the window seat with Mariel, tension pushing her fingers into his palm until their knuckles ache. City lights blink beneath them, each car below a spark traveling toward some unknown calamity.

Mariel breaks the hush. "Lucien... I'm scared. Not for me. For us. There are nights I wonder if the darkness is waiting to take you back."

His voice, always even but never truly cold, wraps around her with the quiet strength of shelter, not armor. "Mariel, you think I haven't feared that too?" He brushes hair from her brow. "There's nothing out there that can steal this—unless I let it happen."

She trembles, just slightly, enough for him to sense the earthquakes beneath her calm. He rocks her against him, city lights blurring between their lashes. "You won't lose me. Not now. Not when we've already survived what should have torn us apart."

Soft footsteps find their way into Darius's living room, where Lila stands beneath the faded yellow glow of a table lamp. An old record crackles—low jazz from another lifetime. Darius offers his hand, silent.

Lila steps into his arms without question, her forehead pressed to his chest as they move in slow circles.

"I used to think love was something to be earned only in calm," he says, his voice barely above the music. "But you gave it to me at my lowest."

She smiles, the shape of it a secret just for him. "You found courage for both of us. We're stronger than anything waiting outside that door."

Their dance carries them away from sabotage and conspiracy, past scars and whispered threats. For these minutes, nothing touches them but warmth and rhythm.

Elsewhere—the candlelit observatory, the stark bedroom, the hush of promise—each couple exchanges tokens: a locket, a leather bracelet, an origami crane, a single rose. Words fall away, leaving a mosaic of embraces, of hearts fused by ordeal and resolve.

In each separate pool of light, the world holds its breath. As midnight edges toward dawn, darkness and hope lie entwined—in this rare, indestructible quiet, where love is the only certainty left.

The Final Confrontation

A black limousine purrs to a stop beneath the halo of hotel lights. The marble steps are slick with anticipation, reflecting sapphire streaks and flashes of silver as paparazzi bulbs ignite. Caius steps out first, his hand extended for Seraphina—her gown sleek, obsidian, the shimmer of sequins catching what little warmth the city night can offer. Photographers shout, lenses clicking in rapid staccato. Caius rarely smiles, but he offers the faintest nod, every inch of him sculpted restraint. Seraphina's fingers curl into his; his protectiveness thrums beneath his skin, beneath the smooth veneer of power.

They sweep up the stairs. Inside, the glittering ballroom stretches wide and high, awash in a palette spun from mythology—cobalt and argent draping the tables, starlit domes painted with constellations arcing above. The scent of lilies and rare orchids rides on circulating gold light. Crystal chandeliers scatter fragments of rainbow across tuxedos and bare shoulders. Conversations rise and dip: the sibilance of foreign tongues, brittle laughter tinged with calculation.

One by one, the rest of the Brotherhood makes their entrance, drawing subtle lines through the opulent crowd. Lucien and Mariel—his eyes hawk-sharp, jaw rigid, Mariel's hand ghosting the constellation tattoo at her wrist, always poised but never easy. Darius's gait is measured, Lila's arm looped through his, her features lit by a quiet grace. Orion appears bristling, raw in a midnight suit, Elara a steadying presence beside him; her gaze sweeps the room, cataloging exits and acquaintances with equal care. Silas moves like water, Hana fastened at his side—both almost silent, vanishing into the crowd's seams.

Across mirrored tables—laden with white birds of paradise, glittering glasses, caviar in crescent dishes—international dignitaries and captains of industry cluster close, their laughter a little too bright. Some noses twitch at the unfamiliar, floral-laced perfume, palms damp on crystal. The orchestral swell hushes arguments under its velvet, but nothing dampens the aura of underlying rivalry; these guests, inured to wealth, sniff for weakness. For tonight, the advantage is illusion. Every compliment bears fangs; every well-practiced smile is armor.

Caius breaks away, his stride unhurried but his eyes cold. The velvet-draped windows reflect a thousand candle-lit silhouettes. Lucien lingers there, hands clasped behind his back.

"Security's holding," Caius begins, his voice pitched low under the music. "But I want eyes everywhere. We can't trust the guest list."

Lucien's reply is clipped, his accent more precise in tension. "Too many unknowns. Garcia's team spotted odd movement by the kitchens. And one of the dignitaries hasn't cleared background."

Caius's mouth twists. "We play the part until it's time," he says. "But nobody leaves your side, understood?"

"Tonight, I trust no one," Lucien murmurs, and inclines his head before fading back.

Nearby, Darius drifts methodically along the periphery, his phone screen glancing with coded messages. Mariel slips to Elara's side as a waiter passes, the glint of a silver tray disguising her whisper.

"I saw two men slip into the south corridor—service lanyards, but the wrong shoes. We're being watched." Mariel's lips barely move; there is strength in her control.

Elara's nod is minute, but her tone is ironclad. "Stay close to Lucien. I'll pass it on."

Meanwhile, Lila and Hana circulate at the edges, faces blessed with practiced composure. They charm politicians, feign interest in a venture capitalist's joke, their eyes always flickering back to their partners. Lila's smile stays steady even as she notes three new arrivals lingering by the west doors, none on her mental list. Hana's fingers tap Morse into the clasp of her clutch: Careful.

Beneath the shimmer, beneath hushed conversation and jazz, a slow unease creeps. Shadows drift among the waitstaff—dark-suited, wrong step, cold eyes belying the crisp uniforms. Someone with security credentials bends to confer with a guest; another guard peels away, vanishing through a door barely cracked in the west hall. Caius feels the coil of danger gathering, tight as wire beneath fine cloth. The illusion of invincibility tastes sharp in the air—a lie gilded in diamond and light.

No matter how dazzling the stage, every man and woman in power here knows the cost: Not one empire is ever truly safe, and fragile respect can vanish with the whisper of a threat. In this world, majesty is always edged with menace. Status hangs by invisible threads, easily severed. This night, all the silk and silver only seem to amplify the sense that everything—wealth, reputation, even love—might shatter on the ballroom's flawless marble with a single misstep.

At the main dais, the Brotherhood—six couples strong now—move as one. Caius meets Lucien's eyes. Orion flexes his left hand, restless. Darius studies the exits, Silas's face unreadable. For an instant, unity hangs between them, silent as a blade. Every sense sharpens. The music swells, impossibly bright and hollow. Guests swirl, champagne flows, but unseen, the shadows draw closer. The night's mask is nearly slipping.

Caius has barely moved from the dais when the world splits open.

A low, vicious rumble tears up through the marble floors—the chandeliers shudder, their crystal drops clinking like glass wind chimes forced into discordant prayer. For a blink, the lights flicker an icy white across velvet and mirrored glass, shadows writhing along every edge of the grand ballroom. Then half of the room falls blank, drowned in night. Screams flood the air, piercing and half-smothered, panic surging like a wave in a storm. Perfume and sweat mingle, the reek of fear replacing the fragranced expectation from moments before.

Caius's mind sharpens as chaos unfurls, a glass pane freezing into perfect clarity. He searches, first for Seraphina—heart thudding at the memory of an ambush years ago when blood meant kin lost forever—then for his brothers. He pulls Seraphina close, fingers firm against her wrist. Guilt snaps at him, the old haunting echo: not quick enough last time, not strong enough. That night carved the scar on his cheek and seeded a resolve no fire could burn away. Tonight cannot end like then.

A volley of staccato pops rattles the illusion of safety as masked figures surge through the vaulted doors. Every movement is blade-sharp—submachine guns glinting under the washed-out ballroom lights, batons swinging with surgical intent. The leader's demand rips across the chaos, guttural and amplified, "Orion Brotherhood! Reveal yourselves!"

Caius's anger rises, cold and purposeful, corralled beneath the skin. He scans for the exits—already sees Darius herding Lila toward shadows, Lucien and Mariel melting behind the bar's mirrored frost, Orion flaring protectively in front of Elara, Silas's silhouette steadying Hana with quiet dignity.

Shouts cut through the bedlam. A guest in silver stumbles into Darius's path, dazzled and useless, her sequined gown catching on a toppled chair. Darius's hand lands on her shoulder with careful force. "That way. Keep low." His voice is an anchor in the surge; Lila darts him a look, all anxious warmth and unyielding backbone, then pulls the guest along the wall.

A shot slams into the plaster nearby. Elara's breath catches as fragments rain over the banquet floor, dust mingling with the sharp tang of spent adrenaline. Orion's eyes fix on her, wild with the need to protect, voice cut raw. "Stay behind me." Elara nods, her hand tight around his, knuckles paling.

"Mariel, now," Lucien murmurs, low and taut. He yanks her behind the bar as another burst sends red wine weeping down the counter. Mariel's mouth hardens, eyes fierce, her mind calculating angles as she presses her back against his chest.

Hana's breath is barely a whisper. Silas leans in, shielding her with his frame as the echoes of boots grow nearer. His pulse hammers beneath his cool veneer, all senses heightened; he catalogs escape routes, attacker formations, the gleam of a gun barrel sweeping their way.

Security agents, earpieces fizzling with static, rally at the ballroom's rear. Two try to direct guests to safety, but second and third concussive blasts from the side hallways slice off every hopeful exit. The scent of singed carpet and ozone blooms as smoke begins to curl in through the half-collapsed arch. Fear is now a taste, bitter and coppery on the tongue.

Caius ducks behind the thick curtain of the stage, yanking Seraphina to his side. Her eyes are wild, mouth set. She moves before he commands her, checking the small pistol hidden in her clutch, scanning the darkened space. Together, they are sharper: Seraphina's courage stoking the fire that Caius locks tight behind his jaw.

"Don't lose me," she breathes, and he nods, every muscle wound. He's back in another half-lit room—years ago, gunsmoke in his lungs, blood on marble—only this time, he knows the cost, has learned when to strike and when to shield. He must not fail her, not them, again.

From the ballroom's epicenter, the lead attacker paces, weapon sweeping side to side. Others peel off, moving methodically toward the Brotherhood's positions, their presence a dark tide closing in.

Seraphina checks their backs. "We need a diversion," she whispers, her body rigid, poised to spring.

"Wait for my signal," Caius commands, not unkindly—reassuring, though the undercurrent of terror knits the space between every word.

Near the mirrored bar, Mariel fumbles for Lucien's hand, grounding herself amid the din. Darius glances behind, every sound parsed for threat, the ghost of that old betrayal flickering through his memory. He draws Lila in close, murmurs something only she can hear; her brow knits, but she doesn't falter.

Bullets thud into columns and marble as the first operatives advance into their zones. Silas tightens around Hana, senses the moment when her fear flares then hardens, turning to steel. These are split seconds stretched thin as glass—each measured move recalls a lifetime of danger, every lesson bought in pain.

Then, from nowhere, the ballroom erupts in a blinding burst of white. A flash grenade cracks, stealing sight and turning every sound into distant thunder. Caius's hand stays locked to Seraphina's. His mind—razor-sharp, flinching from regret—counts heartbeats, holding out against the dark.

Alarms wail into the void, urgent and shrill. The Brotherhood—battered but unbroken—braces for the storm that's only begun.

Gunfire tears across the marble, bright muzzle flashes reflected in the chandeliers and mirrored tabletops. The sweet, heavy scent of crushed orchids mingles with smoke. Caius's voice cuts through chaos, deep and steady even as fractured glass crunches beneath his shoes. "Clear the floor—stairwell, left of the orchestra!" His comm hisses, static-laced, but the Brotherhood security moves, weaving between fallen cutlery and overturned velvet couches.

Seraphina is already in motion, dark hair whipping past her bare shoulders. She glides across shattered crystal and bloody footprints, eyes locked on guests huddled beneath the dais. A pianist sobs near a broken music stand. Seraphina drops to her knees beside a wounded diplomat, her silk gown streaked with red. Her hands are warm, quick. "Hold here, press tight—good. Follow me. Keep low." She sweeps them forward, collecting lives as she goes, her voice an anchor in the gale. A young debutante clings to Seraphina's wrist, smeared lip gloss trembling.

Caius's earpiece crackles. "Main exit blocked," someone growls—Lucien's calm, steel-threaded tone. Cursing, Caius scans the ballroom's gilded dome, the high frescoes spattered now with shrapnel. He can sense his brothers' presence—a pulse beneath the chaos, the echo of old loyalty forged in darker nights. They need no words. They move in concert, the unspoken language of years flowing between drawn glances and sharp gestures.

Lucien, crouched by the ruined wine cart, flicks a lock of damp hair from his brow, eyes narrowing against stinging smoke. "Mariel?" His hand finds hers, grounding them both. Mariel's knuckles whiten over a compact pistol, her lips pressed thin. The gala's tablet glows in her other palm, flickering with blue security code and scrolling feeds. "I've got the digital link. Cut their access from here," she murmurs, her voice little more than a hush drowned in gunfire. Lucien's fingers dance, surgical and sure, navigating firewalls as Mariel scans the crowd, her body shielding him from potential threats. A bullet splinters glass overhead. Mariel presses her shoulder against Lucien's, steady. "Two in the back office—keep going." Lucien nods, keyed into her rhythm. A language of sighs and glances—no wasted effort.

Nearby, Darius and Lila move through swirling smoke, his hand spread across her back. They dart past columns, guiding a trembling cluster of waitstaff toward the kitchens. The acrid haze stings their eyes; overhead, the sprinkler system tick-ticks, refusing to yield. "Garcia!" Darius shouts, voice rough. The security chief emerges, badge askew, breath ragged. "We need the east exit," Lila says, urgent. "Ready?" She locks eyes with Darius—trust, a brief spark. Together they push heavy metal doors closed, barring attackers with the weight of their fear and determination. Garcia radios out as Darius hoists a fallen server's limp body over his shoulder. Lila gathers the rest, her voice calm, almost maternal, directing them through the maze of smoke and broken dishware.

Orion's snarl rips through the chorus of screams as bullets rip into the long banquet table. Elara presses her palm over his, steering his wild energy. "They've got three—hostages by the windows." Orion's muscles tense, heat coiling like a storm beneath his skin. He nods, teeth bared. "Now," Elara whispers. Together, they vault the barricade. Orion crashes into the masked assailants: a crack of bone, a cry of pain. Elara's arms gather a weeping child, fingers brushing fine glass shards from his cheeks. "It's alright, sweetheart. Listen to me, just breathe—look at me." Her voice lulls the panic, and she wraps the boy in her coat. Orion stands over the last attacker, eyes locked with Elara—her faith lending him focus, reeling his fury into sharp purpose.

Up above, on the shadowed balcony, Silas's voice is a whisper at Hana's ear. "Flash, then with me. On three." The gunmen prowl nearby, oblivious. Hana nods, fingers clutching a cold metal canister. She tosses it; there's a burst of light and shouts. Silas melts into the darkness, drawing the kidnappers after him with the promise of prey. He leads them into a narrow storeroom, his footsteps silent over scattered glass. Hana throws the bolt—the hiss of fire suppressant floods the gap beneath the door. Coughing, the assailants collapse. Silas slips an arm around Hana's waist, gratitude a flicker in his cool gaze. "We did it." She squeezes his hand, hope pulsing through the smoke.

Caius catches Seraphina's eye from across the devastation—the flutter of her fingers: safe, moving forward. Their wordless understanding roots him; every action is a thread spinning between these lives, woven by battles before. The team sweeps guests toward the hidden stairwell, each couple working as if rehearsed.

A moment's silence—a heartbeat. Then fresh gunfire erupts, louder and closer. More shadows surge against the light, the air sharp with ozone and panic. The Brotherhood, battered but unbowed, regroups near the ruined ballroom dais. Their actions have carved narrow corridors of safety through the chaos, but the most dangerous threat is still gathering, storming for the heart of their fragile peace.

The ballroom is chaos, fractured by violence and raw with the scent of burning insulation and spilled champagne. Flashes of submachine guns reflect in shattered crystal, their thunder echoing off marble and velvet. Beneath the grand dome painted with constellations—once a vault of promise—fear swirls like vapor around the feet of the desperate and the brave.

Behind the main stage curtain, Seraphina catches the glint of steel, the lead assailant's aim fixed on Caius. Her body acts before thought: she crosses the distance in a blur, the slick silk of her gown tightening about her legs, adrenaline sharpening her senses. The clarity is surgical—she feels the grit of glass beneath her heel, catches the tang of cordite and sweat. Her mind reels with old memories: holding off housebreakers as a teenager, the rattle of rain against a dust-choked window, the sound of her mother's voice warning, always—protect your own, no one else will.

She slams into the attacker, driving him behind the thick velvet. The world narrows to breath and pain and motion—his elbow cuts a path across her scarred forearm, but she barrels through the blow, fingers curling around his wrist and twisting. The snap is sharp, wet, and the gun clatters to the boards. He curses, shoving, but she refuses to yield. She's been forged by too many nights alone; she knows how to be stronger than her fear. She draws on every dawn spent in training, every dark hour spent guarding others when all she wanted was to rest. Her knee drives into his thigh. He falters. She levers his arm back till he screams, and he breaks away, clutching the ruined limb, vanishing into the roiling dark.

She doesn't watch him flee—her eyes find Caius through the gloom, his face blanched with worry and awe. He's not the center of her world; he's her axis—the constant that gives direction to her vortex of purpose and rage.

Not far off, Lucien shoulders his way through a tide of panicked guests, lips pressed flat. Two black-masked men close in on him, guns up, hunting. Mariel—her breath shallow, heart galloping—slips from the shadowed bar with a decanter gripped tight. Glass trembles against sweat-slick fingers. She roars, drawing their blaze; rounds splinter a mirrored pillar and spray her with dust and slivers.

Lucien lunges in, precise and silent. His elbow cracks across the first attacker's jaw. A brief, vicious tangle—then Lucien's knee finds the man's solar plexus, folding him. Mariel, blinking through a haze of terror, brings the heavy glass down on the second's skull. The crunch resounds; pain shoots up her arm. The man slumps, helmet rolling away. Mariel stares—breathless, alive. Over the years, she's kept Lucien grounded, through boardroom betrayals and deals made at bloody cost. Tonight, she shatters her bounds with violence, her devotion acting as shield and sword.

Elsewhere, Darius and Lila dive as scarlet light dances across Darius's chest—a sniper's mark. Lila lands first, the sting of marble bruising her hip. She whips out her flashlight, hands shaking, teeth clenched, finger snapping a coded arc at the waiting guards above the chandelier. The answer is a hiss of suppressed gunfire, a fine rain of crystal dust as the sniper's perch shatters. Darius scrambles up, steadies his hand, and fires a clean shot into the open gap. Memories of whispered sabotage, of lives saved and lost in hospital halls, race through him. Lila's faith in his judgment, her willingness to spill blood for him, is an anchor—together, they're unbreakable.

On the edge of the ruined banquet floor, Orion is a force of fury, every muscle strung tight with the need to protect. Two assailants sweep in, their boots cracking glass, but Orion's vision is tinted red, all sense of reason slippery and distant. Elara pushes through the melee, planting herself in his path, hands cupping his jaw, voice low and sure.

"Orion, look at me. Stay with me. They want chaos—you're more than rage. You're ours."

Her words thread through the scream of alarms and shouts, grounding him. He exhales, chest heaving. He pivots, sudden, precise—elbows one assailant cleanly, catching the other's weapon and driving him down with a practiced sweep. Power, controlled—learned through wounds, held steady by love.

In the smoke and shadow of a storage nook, Hana presses her back to the wall, blood drumming in her ears as the masked figure looms. She holds a broken bottle, glass glittering. The attacker lunges, and she sidesteps, dragging pain from old memories—late-night corridors, Silas's quiet instruction, the promise of her own strength. She hisses defiance, slicing the air, every inch electric with determination.

A crash from outside. Silas barrels in, eyes wild, moving with swift calculation. He knocks the assailant aside, catching Hana's arm. Together, they wrench the attacker down, Hana's knee on his chest, Silas binding his hands with a torn curtain. Their unity, tested by secrecy and silence, sings in the shared breathlessness of survival.

Sirens cut through the smoky dawn, a blue pulse against silver wreckage. City guards pour in, rounding up the reeling remnants of the ambush. Broken chandeliers drip like dew onto the ruined velvet, and the Brotherhood—bloodied, trembling, but defiant—collapse into each other's arms at center stage, bodies pressed close as the gray light of sunrise slips through the fractured windows. For one heartbeat, midnight world and morning hope exist together, and everything that's ever bruised them is remade into something close to triumph.

The Betrayer's End

Beneath the city's heartbeat, in the Brotherhood's chamber cut from polished stone, time seems to hold its breath. Shadows slip along the granite walls, tinted honey-gold by lanterns echoing a night without stars. Each couple stands in solemn lockstep: Seraphina poised at Caius's back, Mariel close behind Lucien, Lila's pale hand gripping Darius's, Elara steady at Orion's side, and Hana a quiet pillar beside Silas. They form an ordered arc around the council's black oak table, the constellation emblem between them glinting with cold clarity—a symbol everyone once trusted.

Lucien's knuckles tighten on his tablet as he steps forward. "The gala's chaos was more than misfortune." His voice is low, words measured, but his eyes flicker with calculation as the chamber's fiber-optic stars blink overhead. He taps the screen, and sharp images stutter to life along the stone—footage spliced, audio clipped, a silhouette lurking in a corridor where none should tread. The edges of his calm are frayed, stitched with frustration barely masked.

Mariel draws nearer, her own evidence clean and inescapable. "Audit logs from last night's breach." She points, her nail gliding to the string of binary fingerprints burned into the data—impossible to refute, unmistakable in their source. "Tampering came from inside. From someone we trusted." Her words hang brittle in the silence, knowledge scraping at old wounds.

Darius sits rigid, scanning the document trembling in his hands. Even the oak table can't ground him now. "Wire transfers to an offshore shell. All authorized under one signature." His voice cracks but does not falter. "These... these funds didn't just vanish. They paid for men, for weapons." Lila's grip anchors him, though her face is chalk-white, and suspicion churns in her stare like stormwater eddying around a drain. No one dares to speak, but heads tilt, eyes narrow, breaths grow shallow. Something sacred fractures in that quiet.

Orion's temper snaps. His fist slams down—a gunshot echo bounding off the stone. The screens flicker. "You want to look us in the eye and explain that?" His voice vibrates with outrage, but the quake beneath is fear—fear that his circle, their family, no longer holds. "Tell us what the hell you've done." The accused meets Orion's glare, lips parted in denial, then pressed tight by guilt bleeding through the mask.

Time slows as the silence grows. Caius feels sweat bead on his brow, the tightness in his chest almost suffocating. Everything he's built roils at the edge of collapse—his empire, his loves, even the myth of his own judgment. Did he miss the signals in his own house, among his own men? Did his craving for control blind him? Doubt claws at him, raw and cold.

The betrayer's voice slips out, at first just a whisper. "I had to. You don't know what it's like—always outside, always waiting for scraps." He shudders, eyes darting over each face, desperate for absolution and finding only horror reflected back. "We built this on a lie, all of us.

Every scar you carry is also mine." Bitterness etches every word, old betrayals surfacing like rot.

Silas moves first, wordless and implacable, Hana shadowing him, their presence hemming the traitor in. The assembly's unity—once their shield—now binds the betrayer in chains. The man sags between them, pride and resistance crumbling in his defeated posture.

Caius lifts his chin, steel laced through every syllable despite the tremor beneath. "You will be confined below until we deem it safe. No more secrets. Not tonight." Two security officers materialize with the hush of well-oiled machinery, their hands neither harsh nor forgiving as they shepherd the fallen council member to the stairwell. The traitor's eyes search for mercy and find none.

Around the table, a silence descends thick enough to breathe. Seraphina's composure gives way; a sob slips through her lips. Caius folds his arm around her, pulling her to his side, and the others watch—some with grief, some with fury, all shaken to the core. The light in the chamber gleams from the table's star-shaped inlay, haloing trembling hands and haunted faces.

No one speaks. Not Orion, knees bouncing with pent-up violence; not Lila, jaw set though tears threaten to spill; not Darius, whose gaze drills holes in the documents before him. Silas stands as a sentry at the door, Hana holding his arm as if to keep him from dissolving into the stone itself. Each person's mind churns with suspicion, regret, and confusion. Even now, loyalty aches but trust will not settle.

Above them, the artificial stars pulse, silent witnesses to a dynasty undone. Something vital has cracked, but as Caius soaks in the devastation, one thing remains—he must not break. If he falls, everything falls. The weight of every love, loss, and oath presses harder as the traitor disappears below, leaving only the echo of betrayal and the indelible possibility of ruin.

A golden hush fills the sitting room as afternoon bends into evening. Light slants in through the high western windows, painting trembling patterns over the pale rug and brushing languid warmth across the faces gathered in a wide, subdued arc. The vast glass glows with the last embers of day, throwing the green of the courtyard's clipped lawn into sharp relief beyond. The air carries the scent of cut grass and, faintly, smoke—echoes of extinguished chaos, memories barely put to rest.

No one speaks. Caius sits at the head of a long, cream linen sofa, his hands folded and heavy atop his knee, as if bracing for a blow. Empty chairs flank the group—sentinels for the fallen, ghosts occupying spaces their humid breaths once did. Lucien's eyes linger on the largest of these absences, his jaw set tight. Orion leans forward on his elbows, staring into nothing, while Silas sits back in the corner shadow, fingers curled and flexing with silent agitation. The air is thick with the ache of things unsaid.

Seraphina's voice wavers first, breaking the stillness. "He brought me coffee every morning," she says, her words small and trembling in the cavernous quiet. "Not for thanks. Only... habit. Even when I worked alone, late, he waited for me to finish." She swallows, her chest rising against an emotion that shows in the press of her fingers at her collar. "The night he died, I asked him to go home early. If I hadn't—" The words choke off. Mariel slides beside her, resting a gentle hand on Seraphina's shoulder. Hana moves next, silent and sure, pressing a handkerchief into Seraphina's palm.

A ripple passes through the group. Mariel glances toward the windows, the light catching her constellation tattoo as she speaks. "He admired you, Seraphina. Said every victory felt like his too. That's what matters. These memories are what will last." Her words land softly, punctuated by the distant sound of birds in the courtyard and the muted drone of the city far below.

Lila draws in a shaky breath. She unwraps a slender ring from a velvet cord, turning its band over between trembling fingers. "He fixed this," she whispers. "When I lost it, he found it in the stairwell and cleaned it for me." Her voice is rain-soaked silk. "It isn't much, but—I promised him I'd wear it always." Darius's hand closes around hers, his knuckles white, his gaze fixed.

"I can't stop thinking about it," Darius lets out, his voice scraped raw. "That someone amongst us could do this. Every lesson in trust feels like a lie tonight. I should have seen it. Should've—" His words fracture. Lila wipes away her tears and shakes her head, squeezing his fingers tighter.

Across the room, Lucien's gaze drops to his lap. The silence that follows is so fragile it almost shatters when he speaks. "I was blind," he says, his words clipped. "There were signs—there had to be. I missed them." Mariel touches his thigh, her words urgent but warm.

"You see too much, Lucien," she says. "Don't forget that. But even you can't read every shadow." She leans her head to his, and for a moment the tension in his shoulders unravels.

Elara's eyes linger on the trembling ring in Lila's hand. She shifts her weight, her voice carrying a gentleness that hushes the room. "Let's do something together," Elara suggests. "A vigil. For those lost. For all of us." She glances outside, to where the jasmine bushes sway in a soft wind. "We'll light candles by the garden."

The group moves outside as one, gathering on the stone pathway threading through untamed blooms. The air outside is brisk, laced with earth, carried on the breath of approaching night. Each partner takes a taper and matches flicker bright gold against the gathering gloom. They stoop to touch fire to wick, the flames trembling uncertainly at first, eager, but easily threatened.

Orion shields Elara's trembling candle from a sudden breeze, his hand cradling hers. "It won't go out," he murmurs. She looks up at him, grateful. Silas and Hana stand side by side, the glow gilding the softness in Hana's eyes as she bows her head, her lips moving in silent prayer.

One by one, voices rise—a recitation of memories, vows, names spoken like incantations meant to anchor the lost to the living. Caius stands at the edge of the circle, his candle a small defiant star. In the flickerlight, grief etches itself into his features: old pain pulled tight across his mouth, the shadow of a scar catching the flame's reflection. He tightens his grip on the candle, sensing the heat sinking into his callused skin. He wills himself not to look away from this mourning, not to retreat behind command. Tonight, the urge to shield, to strategize, wars with the ache to simply be—to feel, to honor, to grieve.

Hana moves last, adding her flame to the line. As dusk deepens, the group closes together around a field of wavering light; some rest their faces on shoulders, some weep without sound. From inside, faint strains of music drift—slow, elegiac chords. The candles flicker beneath the jasmine, their scent heavy, cloying, insistent—a vow that memory, and hope, endure.

The flames gutter, casting shifting stars across faces and hands. Not one of them stands alone.

The chamber glows with low, golden light, the hidden sconces drawing out blue-black shadows that cling to polished granite and echo old secrets. Scattered petals from the jasmine vigil drift beneath heavy boots—a rare softness in this sanctum carved for power and reckoning. The round council table, black oak lacquered to a night's shimmer, occupies the room's heart. Around it, the Brotherhood—five men, five women—converge in new silence, faces drawn by fatigue and smudged candle smoke.

Caius moves with slow purpose, his hand brushing fleetingly against Seraphina's shoulder as if grounding them both. The faint scent of jasmine stirs memories he tries not to taste. He gestures with a nod, commanding presence without a word; one by one, the others settle, their partners standing close—guarded halves of a nearly broken whole.

Silas's voice slices through the air, quiet yet steely. "New protocols," he begins, his pale eyes on no one and everyone, "and nothing made in darkness any longer. We set oversight in cycles—one failsafe after the next. Transparency, even when it hurts. No more silent corners for ghosts." He passes a sharply folded note around the table, his knuckles whitening for just a moment as Hana's hand covers his.

Lucien leans in, jaw set and eyes shadowed by exhaustion. "Encrypted nets. Nothing leaves this room unguarded. I'll oversee the firmware myself." There's grit behind his formality, a stubborn refusal to be taken off-guard again. Mariel, seated at his side, already sketches outlines onto her tablet—her fingers darting deftly as lightning through the legal codes that will become their new oath.

The group draws tighter. Pastries gone untouched sweeten the air with almond and cardamom, a jarring reminder of easier nights. Orion's hand meets Darius's in a tight, brief shake—a signal in the exchange, aggression tempered with apology. Lila leans close to Hana, her whisper only barely a syllable, passing a hope or a fear between them. Seraphina crosses the space between herself and Mariel, her embrace fierce and lingering, her hair brushing Mariel's cheek. In these small gestures, something mends: not forgiveness, not yet, but a cautious willingness to patch ragged edges.

Caius steadies himself. He feels the table's carved emblem beneath his palm—the constellation whose points were almost scattered for good. He looks—really looks—at each pair, cataloguing the rawness behind their eyes. Orion's harsh energy, only just unreadable; Darius's vigilance overlaying a soul lastingly bruised. Silas's barely perceptible tremor as he releases Hana's hand, as if distance could finally loosen the knot of guilt inside him. Each woman by their side keeps the balance; he sees, for the first time maybe, how much of this fragile unity rests on those threads.

He breathes in, slow and deliberate. The jasmine lingers, threading memory with possibility. "We move forward—never blind to what's behind us." His words come low, almost rough, but every syllable lands with certainty. "We stand together. But this—" he taps the edge of the constellation—"remains only if we remember: doubt is not a curse. It keeps us honest."

Seraphina's eyes shine, her lips pressed tight. She holds herself fiercely, ready to defend or to crumble if one gust blows too hard. Lucien's hand finds Mariel's beneath the table, squeezing once, as if to say forgive, forgive. Darius stands with his arm loose around Lila, who tries and fails to hide the red around her eyes.

A hush pulses in the space. For a beat, no one moves. The air is fragile: hope balanced on the edge of exhaustion, unity haunted by loss.

"You trust it, then?" Orion's voice is a ragged growl, one eyebrow arching, skepticism naked in his tone.

"I trust this more than I trust fear," whispers Silas, his voice barely more than breath. "It's all we've got left."

"Trust is what they tried to burn from us," Lila says softly, her words like the hush of night wind, "but we're not ashes yet."

"Well, I could use a few less surprises," Lucien mutters, drawing a rueful snort from Darius. Mariel squeezes his shoulder in silent comfort.

"Then don't get too comfortable," says Orion. "Comfort got us here."

"It won't again," Caius replies, his voice steel sliding through honey. "We're changed. And we'll hold to that. Even if it hurts."

One by one, the others nod. Not eager, but resolved. Through the window's slit, city lights scatter themselves like jewels, the pattern uncanny—points mirrored above in the fiber-optic sky the chamber ceiling wears like hope's armor.

Caius lets himself feel the weight—of their trust, of their fear, of what's left to lose. He knows unity's a promise stitched with scars, not guarantees. But as the Brotherhood rises together, a wary constellation in the hush, he hopes the darkness outside will find them less easy to fracture. For tonight, they hold. For tonight, the light—the love, the doubts, the strength won from agony—binds them, and the future waits, trembling on the other side of the glass.

Burning the Oath

Caius enters first, shoulders squared beneath the weight of memory, boots thudding on stone that drinks in every echo. The council chamber's circular vault rises around him, filled with a silence too dense for comfort. Overhead, fiber-optic points shimmer in the black, imitating constellations that once governed their fates. Amber sconces burn in their brackets, throwing out pools of warm light that drag shadows longer and darker onto the granite walls—walls that gleam with veiled secrets and betrayals. One last time, Caius takes his place at the blackened oak table, its surface marked by a thousand unspoken promises and threats. Beside him, Lucien's hands are clasped so tightly that his knuckles pale. Darius sits opposite, still as a sculpted sentinel; Orion leans in, restless, tension flickering across his jaw; Silas stands just outside the circle of light, eyes turned inward, the picture of a man who has learned to trust nothing, not even the dusk.

Around the room, each couple finds a corner of solace. Seraphina's hand is light but grounding on Caius's forearm, her thumb tracing the old scar. Mariel's body gently tilts toward Lucien, her gaze steady, lips a thin line betraying nerves and resolve. Lila's fingers interlace with Darius's, a silent tether binding them to hope. Elara presses close to Orion, steadying his breath with her own calm. Hana's palm settles on Silas's shoulder, drawing him a little nearer to home, a subtle promise rooted in gentleness. The chamber quietly reflects their gathering, granite polished to the point of a mirror, glinting with fragments of a past bartered for power.

Seraphina is the first to move, the hush parting around her as she rises. Her voice ghosts out, low and strong, laced with old fire. "Thank you, shadows. You kept us alive. But you took too much. I refuse your shelter now—there's nothing left for us here." In the pause her words leave, a frail reverberation stands—a ripple of gratitude, but also of mourning. One by one, each woman names the darkness that stalked her: Mariel speaks of silent betrayals buried in data and locked doors, Lila remembers faces lost to ambition, Elara's whisper is strong enough to shatter self-doubt, and Hana is barely audible but as certain as steel. Their confessions ring out, filling the chamber until the air vibrates with hard-won release—sorrow, but also relief, slick as tears still drying on their cheeks.

A box, nondescript except for the grain of its mahogany, is set before them now. Caius opens it, fingers trembling—not from uncertainty, but from the sharpness of farewells. He passes out the tokens. To Silas, the signet ring—heavy and gold, its crest faded, a relic of first allegiances and promises sworn in blood. To Darius, his coded ledger—pages thin as ash, inked with the cost of lives and fortunes spent to maintain equilibrium that never truly existed. Orion's crimson ribbon, once a marker of victory, now threads between his callused fingers, its color echoing too many nights tinged with regret. To Lucien goes the chess piece, a black knight, weighted with old schemes and sacrifices played two moves ahead, but always at great personal loss. Finally, Lucien passes Caius the torn white card—a piece of the original oath, its edges ragged from countless hidden hands.

In a circle—no order, no designated master—each steps forward to the waiting brazier. Silence is deeper now, breathing with the pulse of flames not yet born. Seraphina leans close to Caius, her gaze fierce and tender all at once.

"Ready?" she murmurs.

He offers a brittle, half-smile. "Never. All the same—it's time."

Lucien's fingers flick the match. The sulfur bite stings the air; the tiny flame leaps, wild. For a second, everyone stares—the future balanced on the cusp of combustion. Caius drops his card in. The flames catch, licking at old parchment, consuming words that once held men in check. One after the other, each relic is added—the ring, the ledger, the ribbon, the knight—their histories swallowed by rising fire. Shadows leap, twisting across the granite, bathing faces in uneasy gold. Caius watches the flames devour every symbol, his heart beating in time with the pops and hisses.

He remembers: the first blood spilled in the name of protection, alliances forged over whiskey and threats, Seraphina lying fragile in his arms after the attack—her breath raw with agony, his certainty shattering. He thinks of nights spent rooting out betrayal, his fingers stained by secrets, his soul growing heavier with each act of survival. Yet, as the last token blackens, a strange lightness creeps in—guilt softened by the presence of Seraphina's hand in his, sorrow cut by faint hope. Her love is a flame that doesn't destroy but illuminates parts of him that power never reached.

Smoke unspools, blue-gray and dense, rising toward the simulation of stars above. Resignation mixes with resolve, grief with release. When the last charred scrap collapses inward, a hush falls. None move. The air is thick with the scent of scorched velvet, old paper, and the faint tang of spent wax. Each face is transformed in the fire's last glow—haunted, yes, but resolute, eyes fixed not on defeat, but on the unmapped future waiting beyond those ancient granite walls.

The room is all sun-blind gold—a stark contrast to the deep-shadowed silence of the chambers below. Floor-to-ceiling windows stretch along one side, glass still cool to the touch as radiant light pools in, spilling across the oval-glass table where old power once whispered in darkness. Now, that power glints coldly in the open, no longer veiled. Caius sits at the curve, shoulders squared but hands loose on his knees, Seraphina beside him, resting her palm atop his, the light catching the edge of his scar; so many years, so much hidden in shadow.

Lucien bends over a slim tablet, fingers drumming against its mirrored screen. Mariel sits to his left, posture crisp, pen poised, her eyes scanning Lucien's notes before glancing out the window. Instead of cold marble or the silent threat of closed doors, the conference room breathes—leather, sunlight, wax from last night's spent candles, and the faintest undertone of cut grass drifting up from the gardens. The others complete the circle: Darius, broad and thoughtful, hand entwined with Lila's; Orion's restless foot tapping, Elara anchoring him with a touch to his thigh; Silas, quiet as ever but standing now, Hana by his side, calm.

No one speaks for a breath. A low pulse of tension hums between them, charged not with secrecy but anticipation.

Lucien looks up. "We start with the new archive. No more blind accounts, no more coded siphons. Every dollar, every deal—traced, open. Full digital ledger, public record, every transaction cross-checked by three independent firms we don't own. Risky?

Extremely." The faintest arch of his eyebrow, a challenge. "But it's the only way forward if our name is ever to mean more than a whispered threat."

Mariel's voice is low and clear. "Transparency must be more than numbers. Every research protocol, every clinical trial, every patent—open access. We build trust by offering proof, not promises."

Caius watches them. His pulse pounds against the bones of his wrist, all muscle memory craving the temptation of half-truths, vaults, and coded messages. He imagines—can almost feel—how daylight leaks through every lock he's ever trusted. The cost: vulnerability, the inability to shield, to predict. Yet here, Seraphina's fingers curl tighter around his. He finds steady breath.

A dialogue block:

"I don't need to tell you how old-guard elites will react to this," Darius says, keeping his voice measured. "They'll say we're capitulating, giving them a blueprint for their own downfall."

Orion's lip curls, tapping the table. "Let them talk. Let them stare. For once, it's us setting the rules. Not them, and not whoever's lurking behind the next closed door."

Lila squeezes Darius's hand, her gaze steady. "If we're honest about our mistakes, the narrative changes. We show them power isn't about controlling shadows."

Silas shifts, rising. His voice is softer than the others expect, steady as stone. "All remaining covert branches—mine included—are dissolved. I manage liquidation. The proceeds go to foundations...for the city, for every life our silence damaged." He glances at Hana, quietly handing her a slim folder brimming with final numbers. "No more walls."

Hana meets his gaze—her pen moves, script precise as she records each pledge. "Every commitment, written. No loopholes."

Elara unfolds a map, spreading it with graceful, deliberate movement. Darius moves closer, palms pressing to edges. Together, their hands mark the city: red dots for support centers, green circles for neighborhoods most fractured by war-like skirmishes of their old order. The paper is dotted with names, places they know and some they've learned the hard way.

"We start outreach immediately," Elara says quietly. "Counseling, real support—not just money. We have to show up, even when it costs us."

Darius's tone softens. "We owe them that. Maybe more."

Around the glass table, plans build like scaffolds—fragile, shining, held up by hope and the tension of history. Lucien scrolls through projections, and Mariel annotates strategies for medical transparency and community partnership. Silence isn't emptiness—it's the aching stretch of possibility.

Outside, the city is waking—a spatter of car horns, the distant bleary call of a fruit vendor, the world still unsure whether to believe in dawn. Inside, the Brotherhood's decision cracks centuries' worth of coded deals and closed-door betrayals. In the city's skyline, old adversaries will see exposure as weakness, a beckoning vulnerability. Some will plot retaliation; others, perhaps, will watch and wonder if power can thrive without threat. Their empire's bones—once steel and secrecy—now offer themselves to daylight, and with it, to judgment. This is how legacies break and what rises, if anything, is yet unwritten.

But within Caius, conviction grows sharper than fear. He remembers the heat of firelit stone, the scent of Seraphina's hair in the middle of catastrophe, how easily love withers in the cold of secrets. For years, the only way to keep his world safe has been to hide. Today, he feels something riskier—hope. To trust his brothers, his lover, and the city to see the best he can offer, not just the worst he could hide. Maybe legacy is not steel, but light.

A dialogue block:

Seraphina leans in, her voice soft but unflinching. "Let them come. We do this together or not at all. I'd rather face their whispers in the open than suffocate under another secret."

Caius cracks a small, tired smile. "You're braver than any of us."

She matches his gaze. "No, just stubborn enough to believe you're right."

As the group votes—wordless nods, hands brushing hands—a sense of purpose finally settles. Sunlight cuts the last of the shadows away.

Night's embrace lingers as the ten leave behind the hollow-lit chambers, drifting across dew-damp stone and into the hush of the garden. The estate's grounds glisten with a silvery sheen, the lawns jeweled with fresh drops that cling to every blade and petal. Far off, the city hums its midnight lullaby—muffled sirens, distant laughter, invisible to all but the air itself. Overhead, ancient constellations burn against velvet, sharp and impossibly bright. The scent of earth and newly opened jasmine hangs thick, threaded with the sweetness of cut grass and the dark musk of old wood. Every step feels like shedding a skin.

Under the outstretched arms of oaks whose trunks remember centuries, Caius halts. His fingers find Seraphina's, rough against her steady warmth. Moonlight picks out the scar that broke his childhood, the lines that shaped his days. For a heartbeat, the world is only them—their breath crystallizing in the cool, star-fed air.

He lowers his voice, brittle and earnest. "No more secrets between us. Not from today. You get every truth. Every scar."

Seraphina's grip tightens, her voice a breath of fire in the hush. "I didn't stand beside your shadow to fade into it. I want all your light—good and fierce and flawed." She leans in, nose brushing his, her voice a vow. "No more hiding. I'm here, always, and nothing will drag me behind you again."

The others drift in their own orbits. Lucien turns, gaze fixed on Mariel, his silhouette angular in the scattering glow. His fingers clutch hers, as if afraid she'll slip from his grasp. "I kept the world out," he says, mouth set, eyes unbearably soft. "Tried to keep control, and I nearly lost us both. From now on, it's honesty. No more walls."

Mariel's reply is a whisper, reaching deep. "We build this together, Lucien. Even on the days I fear what the world might see. I won't run from what hurts. Not if it means we're facing it together." She rests her forehead against his, radiating steadiness.

Darius and Lila stand just behind a bed of damp irises. Lila strokes his wrist where old wounds hide beneath his shirt. "I promise," she murmurs, "to show you the hope I see in you, even when you can't find it yourself."

Darius's smile is halting, gentle. "I'll never let shadows fall on you without fighting them first. My strength is yours."

Near the garden wall's low stones, Orion squeezes Elara's hand, his thumb tracing lazy circles. "I used to think I had to hold the storm back alone. I'm done being that fool."

Elara tugs him close, her laugh barely a ripple. "Good. Because you're not alone, and I like you much better when you let me stand at your side."

Silas, his silhouette carved by silver and shadow, faces Hana. His voice is barely there. "Every secret I kept was out of fear—of losing you, losing myself. I don't want to be that man anymore."

Hana brushes a strand of hair from his face, her touch patient. "We'll write this new story—one you don't have to live behind locked doors."

Darius pulls a folded relic from his inner pocket: the Brotherhood's old oath, edges charred, script barely readable. Passing it to Orion, its weight tinged with all their years, he lets it go. Orion clears his throat, voice steady. "Strength in unity, whatever the light reveals, whatever the dark conceals." He glances at Elara. "No more."

Elara takes the brittle paper, eyes shining. She rips it—clean and unceremonious—the pieces fluttering like dark moths that can't find flame. Hana steps forward, drawing a scroll of pristine parchment, her delicate script gleaming by moonlight. One by one, they gather—shoulders brushing, hearts exposed—words rising together: "We pledge ourselves to openness, unity, and trust. We are not the shadows we once served, but the light we now choose." Each hand etches a name, ink glistening in the new night. Silas finishes, drawing a tight ring of stars, the unbroken infinite line encircling them all.

The group lingers, hands entwined, gazes lifted. Overhead, their celestial emblem blazes—stars webbed in a lattice only they can truly read. Someone inhales, catching the sharp-green breath of the garden, the metallic tang of ink and paper, the spicy trace of Seraphina's perfume. Old pain recedes, replaced by something weightless—a promise stretching from skin to soul.

No one speaks as they step into the grass, bare feet pressing life into the soft earth. Dawn flickers at the edge of the horizon, starlight mixing with the pink suggestion of morning. Together, partners and friends, they walk forward. The air shivers, sweet and cold, as shadows fall behind them and everything ahead waits, new and unbroken.

Constellations of Fate

Jasmine spills over the old stone bench where Caius and Seraphina sit, their shadows bleeding into the deepening dusk. The sweetness of the blooms rides the breeze—soft, intoxicating, tangled with the cool breath of evening and the memory of distant fires. Lanterns flicker low along the mossy flagstones, casting pools of amber light that never quite chase the darkness away.

Caius's fingers curl tightly around the edge of the seat, knuckles white and scar-ridged along his hand. He draws in a long breath, the air thick with the mingled sharpness of green vine and night-blooming petals. His gaze finds Seraphina's; her profile, framed in gold by the sinking sun, aches with something he feels but cannot name.

"I can still see it," his voice breaks the hush, low and hoarse, edged with gravel from too many sleepless nights. "Smoke along the glass, shots carving up the quiet... Your blood on the marble. For a second, I thought—" He stops, biting down hard on the words, as if naming the fear would conjure it anew.

Seraphina's hand seeks his, tracing the raised scar with a feather's touch. Her fingers are steady, warm, grounding him as the distant chatter of the koi pond and the rustle of leaves close in on their little world. "But you came for me. Through everything—through every wall built to keep us safe—only love stayed standing." She squeezes once, the pressure careful, fierce.

He wants to believe in her certainty. In the quiet, the world presses down—a weight of history: the old wounds, the battered trust, the blood spilled for loyalty and empire. Every scar carries a memory of what he failed to save and the knowledge that despite the power he hoards, fate slips through even closed fists.

Lucien stands a few paces off, his silhouette etched in fading light, posture loose but watchful. A cool breeze plays with Mariel's hair as she leans on the low garden wall beside him. Her constellation tattoo glows, catching the last slice of dusk. The scent of cut grass and earth sharpens behind her.

"After the blackmail... you listened. You didn't doubt me—even when it could have cost you everything," Mariel says, her words almost lost in the murmur of distant water and swaying branches.

"That trust... it wasn't easy," Lucien confesses, reaching to tuck a stray curl behind her ear. "But you're the only one I can't second-guess. You healed more than you know."

Their hands remain close, never quite interlocking—a habit born of restraint and the knowledge that touch, once broken, is never the same. The garden, for all its flowering calm, is fraught with secrets, rooted in the earth like old sins.

Across the lawn, by the water's edge where koi move like liquid rubies, Darius sits cross-legged. His suit jacket is folded on a rock, sleeves rolled above old scars. Lila's head rests easily on his shoulder;

she breathes in jasmine and the faint tang of pond water, eyes closed in trust. Darius traces idle circles over her arm.

"The sabotage… it almost broke me." His confession pools quietly between them, swallowed by the soft rippling of water. "But you're the anchor, Lila. I only weathered it because you never turned away."

Lila lets out a trembling breath. "Fear's only power is making us forget what matters most. I won't let it decide how we live—not anymore."

He nods, drawing her closer, heart beating steadily beneath her ear, reminding him of what was nearly lost and what he has chosen to protect.

At the garden's edge, Orion is a restless shape, his arm tense around Elara. He stares into the darkening treetops, jaw clenched. "I keep seeing Nova lying there—her breathing, so thin, like she was already leaving the world behind." The words come painfully, his voice nearly undone.

Elara's grip finds his—gentle, unyielding. "You didn't let her go. You didn't let *us* go. Your courage was more than chaos. You turned back from the edge, and I found you there. I always will."

Orion shuts his eyes, drawing strength from her touch as the wind shivers through the branches, scattering petals at their feet.

The garden falls to near silence but for the chorus of insects and the whisper of the pond. Shadows gather thick as ink, but the warmth of the five couples pulses bright—an unlikely constellation drawn upon ancient stone, their stories mapped in every quiet glance and lingering hold.

Caius, cocooned in the hush, feels legacy pressing in—from old wounds, from choices made out of fear and love alike. Yet for the first time, hope leaks into the cracks. Could there be a life beyond vigilance, beyond the iron grip of what he stands to lose? He's seen the cost of closing himself to feeling—brother's blood, a woman's near-silence, nights haunted by things unsaid.

One by one, hands find each other, threading through anxiety and relief. The hush deepens, jasmine scent drifting, petals trembling as the breeze stirs. They stand together, eyes catching the last milky trace of light above, and in that shared silence lies a pledge—unspoken, unbreakable—that whatever night comes, love remains, burning steady as the stars above.

The night breathes cool and rich in the garden, the hush broken only by cicadas and the soft murmur of feet in dew-soaked grass. The firepit at the heart of the grounds flickers to life, casting circles of gold and amber onto familiar, shadow-lined faces. Each couple drifts into the loose ring—hands finding waists, shoulders, the solid heat of palms. Above them, the sky stretches pure and cloudless, a broad sweep of blue-black scattered with trembling stars.

Seraphina is the first to glance upward. The fire glints on her cheekbones as she points into the vault of night, her voice low but irrepressible.

"Look—there. Do you see it, just beyond Orion's Belt?"

For a heartbeat, everyone squints into the darkness. Then the new constellation appears—five bright points, luminous enough to outshine their neighboring stars, arranging themselves in a pattern that echoes the five sets of silhouettes encircling the fire. Elara's lips part; Lucien's hand tenses protectively around Mariel's. The group draws in closer, each couple instinctively angling to find their place in the pattern above. Lila traces the air and laughs softly, weaving Darius's fingers through hers.

"Five pairs," Mariel murmurs, wonder shading her words. "It's uncanny. Almost as if it was... waiting for us."

Orion cracks a grin, the firelight smearing warmth across the sharp lines of his face. "Not fate. We earned our place up there—fighting, clawing our way clear of the dark."

"And finding each other," Elara adds, her eyes wet and shining. "Not just up there. Right here."

The constellation lingers, brightening. The night itself seems to pause, listening.

Hana rises, slender and certain, lit on one side by flame, the other by starlight. Silence enfolds her. She speaks not with volume, but with steady grace, her gaze never flinching from the fire, her words soft as velvet.

"In the worst of the night, when every way seemed closed... it was love that gave us direction. One look, one touch—enough to remind us we weren't truly lost." Her voice wavers as she meets Silas's eyes, then strengthens, gaining weight and resonance. "We learned that when the outside world turned cruel—when we couldn't trust even the ground beneath us—we could trust this. Each other. No one here survived alone."

Seraphina's lashes are damp, but she tilts her chin, fiercely proud. Lucien's stoicism cracks, an appreciative nod crossing toward Hana. Darius lets out a long, measured breath, and Lila squeezes his hand, her eyes full of unspoken gratitude.

Silas's shadow stretches tall as he too stands beside Hana. For a moment, words fight him—but then, with a visible surrender, he lifts his chin and lets the truth rise.

"I thought control was strength. That I had to protect, to hold on, never let anyone see the cracks." The flames throw erratic light across his scars, his eyes raw and exposed. "But letting go—trusting Hana's strength—made me better. Not weaker. I don't think I knew how fierce love could be until I risked showing her who I really am."

Hana's hand threads through his. The group holds a collective breath, the moment dense with everything they've lost and won, the air scented with burning wood and garden blooms crushed underfoot. Somewhere, a night bird calls—a clear, uncertain note, and Silas manages a quiet, crooked smile.

One by one, they move—retrieving white candles nestled into a row of stones edging the path. Their hands tremble, just a little, as if recalling all the times when shaking hands meant fear or loss; tonight, the trembling is hope.

Caius, so often first into the storm, presses a lighter to Seraphina's wick. She bows her head, her hair curtaining the faint scar on her arm. Lucien leans toward Mariel, careful—gentle as he brushes her fingers and lights her flame. Darius steadies Lila's candle, the two of them sheltered momentarily in an aura apart from the rest. Orion's broad hand cradles Elara's palm, fire reflecting in his storm-colored eyes as her wick kindles in the steady glow. Silas and Hana complete the circuit, the smallest flame, but impossibly bright against the darkness.

The flames grow, their light knitting the group together. Each face grows distinct—shadowed brows sagging in relief, lips curving into tentative smiles, eyes shining with memories and futures tangled. The garden disappears, replaced by this glowing circle.

They leave the candles on the rim of the firepit, the flames pushing against the night. Above, the constellation blazes in silent accord. The air is thick with jasmine, wood smoke, and the salt of old tears. The Brotherhood's newest legacy isn't in marble towers or contracts inked in secret rooms—it's here, in a ring of starlight and candlelight, faces made golden beneath a sky that—for once—holds only promise.

A hush settles over the garden as dawn breaks, washing the world in shades of pale gold and rose. The air is cool, carrying the ghost of last night's jasmine, dew clinging to the grass and painting the worn stones with silver. Caius stands first, the line of his silhouette clean and resolute, his hand tightening just so on Seraphina's. Around him, the circle forms—ten hands joined, fingers woven as if to anchor them all against what might come. Above, the sky glows. Shadows slip away.

Caius looks to Seraphina, his own reflection written in the gentle lines around her eyes. He speaks, his voice rougher than he intends. "I vow transparency, even when the truth is jagged. I'll lead with courage, not with fear. I'll love you—love all of you—without reservation. That's the order of my world now." His thumb grazes Seraphina's knuckles, a private promise steeping in a public oath.

One by one, partners turn to face each other in that quiet, crystalline morning—the hour where new things are permitted life. Lucien's arms fold Mariel close as he draws a soft breath. His words are low, shaped by years of caution: "No more walls, Mariel. I promise to let you see every scar. Yours are not a burden. They're the reason I believe in us." Mariel's reply is a subtle nod, her fingertips tracing the constellation on her own wrist, that silent assurance that she receives what he offers.

Darius's hand covers Lila's heart, steady and warm. "Whatever chaos comes, we stand steady. You're my center, Lila—our future is built on that." The scent of koi pond water and crushed grass lingers. Lila presses close, her lips barely moving: "No fear, not anymore." Her smile carries tiredness and triumph in equal measure.

Orion can't hold still; every muscle in his frame hums against the dawn. His jaw clenches, then softens. "Elara. I can't swear I'll never falter, but I swear you'll always have the truth of me. Even the parts I'd rather burn away." Elara's hand finds his cheek, her thumb skimming the scar that marks him. Her reply is a whisper meant only for him, but the others hear its echo in her eyes—absolute, unwavering faith.

Hana and Silas stand apart, faces illuminated by the faintest blush of sunlight. Silas's exhale is almost a confession. "No more hiding, Hana. I won't vanish behind control. Vulnerability is the legacy I want to leave you." Hana squeezes his palm, her own voice liquid velvet. "Love lets us be seen—even when the world is sharp."

The vows ripple outward: not proclamations, but incantations. Promises woven between heartbeats that will bind them stronger than law.

Lucien clears his throat, drawing the circle's attention with a new energy. "Let's commit to gathering—face to face—every month. We bear our wounds together; we find solutions together. That's our future."

Mariel, quiet but sure, adds, "I can assemble a new charter for us. Charts, codes—something open, something we shape together." Darius and Elara exchange a glance, the memory of storms in their eyes. Darius says, "We'll coordinate resources, so no one ever stands alone." Elara simply nods, assured and determined. Hana, her words measured and soft, suggests, "Let's join our strengths for causes beyond ourselves. Charitable work. A legacy larger than power or secrecy."

Orion leans into Elara, their shoulders brushing as if to say: We survived the breaking point, and this is the proof.

Their words ring with quiet conviction as promises are gifted around the circle—no longer billionaire titans, but kin chosen by fire and vow. Orion speaks first, his voice ragged but certain: "Honesty, even when it costs. I promise you that." Elara brushes her lips against his cheek, grounding the vow into flesh.

Lila squeezes Darius's fingers. "We anchor each other, always." Her touch pulses with memory and hope, as much a promise as any spoken word.

Silas's mouth curls at the edge, almost a smile. "No more running—no more secrets between us, any of us." Seraphina, her gaze alight as embers, promises Caius: "I choose courage, every time—with you, beside you."

A silent accord knits itself in the first heartbeat of the sun above the firepit. Then, at Caius's gentle prompt, the group ascends the quiet slope behind the garden, shoes brushing the fragrant, dew-heavy grass, until all ten pause atop the rise. Below, the estate's homes glow, windows blazing amber and gold. The lights arc around the hill—five beacons answering the stars overhead. Above, the constellation blazes, impossibly mirrored. Below, the houses echo it—a chain of lights binding the land.

In that moment, dawn paints the group's faces with molten gold, edges softened, shadows erased. They stand together, wordless and watchful, claiming the new day as their own. Overhead, the constellation lingers, patient and eternal. The promise of everything they have chosen, and everything they still might be.

Epilogue

Dawn broke gently over the estate, a wash of gold chasing away the night. Ten figures stood together on the rise, their faces carved in light, their shadows erased. The constellation above mirrored the chain of glowing homes below—an eternal reflection of everything they had fought for.

They said nothing. They didn't need to. The silence itself was a vow.

For though enemies had fallen, though betrayals had been unmasked, the Brotherhood's greatest legacy was not power or wealth—it was love that endured through fire, loyalty that defied death, and hope that no darkness could unmake.

Above them, the stars lingered, patient and eternal. And for the first time, the Orion Brotherhood did not just survive the night—they claimed the day.

Final Thoughts

When I began this journey, I only imagined one story, one dark romance. But the Brotherhood grew into six lives, six loves, six battles that became constellations, each star burning brighter because of you, the readers who walked this path with me.

This final book is not just an ending—it's a promise. That even in betrayal, there can be redemption. That even in despair, there can be devotion. And that the stories we carry—of love, power, sacrifice—never truly end, they only echo on in those who believe.

Thank you for letting me share these men, these women, these broken hearts that dared to heal. The Orion Brotherhood may close here, but its light will remain. And whenever you look up at the night sky, remember: you, too, are part of the constellation.

— Ck Franco

Review Request

Or type this link into your browser:
https://www.amazon.com/review/create-re-view?asin=B0DG3RYZDB